Prologue

Listen. I'm about to give y'all a little glimpse inside my past sexcapades. Emphasis on past ok? The majority of you are here, because you follow me on social media and couldn't wait for me to spill the tea. Now all of these short stories have truth in them. I won't confirm nor deny what the actual truth is, and what's added fiction. Only the parties involved know the truth. The names of all the characters have been changed to protect them. It isn't because they're innocent, it's just that at the time they had girlfriends, a wife, a husband or were special to me. However, let me add that there's no one from my past that I still want presently. Y'all can have those problems. This is my first published novel, and I'm sensitive about my shit. So y'all be nice about it, and I'll add more books soon.

Table of Contents

Chapter 1 : Rona and Chill 1

Chapter 2 : The comedy show 14

Chapter 3 : Boffum 36

Chapter 4 : DADDY 51

Chapter 5 : Elevator Rendezvous 67

Chapter 6 : Her 76

Chapter 7 : Not in the mood 88

Chapter 8 : Married Man 95

Chapter 9 : Possibilities 107

Chapter 1

RONA AND CHILL

We were six weeks into this corona virus pandemic, and I was super stressed. I was thankfully able to work from home during this time. The thing that sucked the most were all these zoom meetings, emails and presentations I had to put together every other day it seemed like. The upside was never having to leave home, and fight traffic or get dressed in work appropriate attire. I was finished daily by 5:30. I was in bed trying to wind down every night with my white wine by 8. One particular night, it was around 11:00 and I wasn't the least bit tired. I was flipping back and forth between the social media apps on my phone. Twitter was dead and IG wasn't popping at all. I wasn't in the mood for the energy on Facebook. I decided to hop on this dating app that I had installed a few days prior. I liked this app because I actually had to make the first move. We could both swipe right, but if I didn't message him first, he couldn't contact me. That made me feel good about doing this. I had heard so many horror stories about online dating apps and I was super apprehensive. I'd like a couple guys, but I hadn't matched with anyone special yet. Hmmm. The next profile I came across was this cute guy that looked to be

Hispanic, or mixed, or maybe even black with light skin. He didn't use an alias, or at least I didn't think so. Daniel was the name on his profile. That didn't sound like an alias to me. My dating profile name was definitely an alias. I just didn't feel comfortable ever putting my real name on any site. The glasses he had on gave him a distinguished Clark Kent look, Just darker. His profile described him as an open minded, laid back, sometimes shy introvert looking for a certain type of energy. That last part intrigued me. I'd been saying that I was more attracted to energy than a certain aesthetic for quite some time. He said he wasn't on here much, but he checked it every 24-48 hours usually. He had a decent job it looked like, nice car, no kids, and he liked to travel. A great smile, nice arms, a great back, and a few fire tats. You could tell he worked out but he wasn't a gym rat. Picture a guy that went to the gym daily faithfully, fell off for 6 months, and now he's back on it. He was solid around his middle and I liked that. Thick is how I'd describe him. The gyms were closed now anyway. I was a plus size girl myself, with DDs, sepia toned skin, and long legs. I loved rocking my protective styles, and minimal makeup, and I loved every ounce of me. Obviously he did too, and the hundreds more that stayed in my DMs on social media but I digress. I swiped right and laid there daydreaming about this guy like a fool. I snapped out of it, sent out a few tweets on Twitter, made sure my doors were locked, and blew my candles out and fell asleep.

    When I woke up the next morning, I had a notification that he and I had matched. I felt that I would look hella thirsty if I messaged him right away, so I put my phone down, and focused on working for the next few hours. It was after lunch when I picked up my phone again. I sent a quick, "Hi, how are you?" message. He answered right away. The small talk was cute for a few minutes. He was also working from home. He had to get back to a meeting and asked if he could give me his number. I usually didn't give or accept numbers so quickly, but for right now I didn't feel any weird vibes, so I said ok. I also liked that he'd asked instead of just sending it. Which is exactly what so many did. He sent it and I smiled. I put it in my phone but didn't put his name in my phone yet. Every time I saved a dude's name in my phone, they started showing their ass. I definitely wanted to see where Mr. Daniel was gonna take this.

Two hours later, I hit him with the "H"" text. He liked it and asked if he could call. For a few minutes, I felt apprehension, because I was nervous, and I hoped he wasn't meaning FaceTime. I didn't feel cute enough right now for all that. Still, I responded back with ok. A full minute passes, and my phone rings. I give it 2 rings, and I answer. It's a regular voice call and not FaceTime. I sigh with relief.

"Hello."

"You definitely sound sexier than I imagined. How are you?"

I'm blushing and smiling my ass off right now. I start to pace, but I don't wanna sound out of breath, so I sit.

"You're a pleasant surprise too. I don't know what I was expecting you to sound like, but it wasn't this."

"Some people say I sound like a black dude with a slight accent in there somewhere."

I laughed. *"That's accurate. I do hear a slight accent. Where are you from?"*

"I was born in Puerto Rico. My mom was born in Dominica, and my dad was born in Puerto Rico. They got married and lived in Puerto Rico until a little after I was born. We moved to Miami and stayed. I moved up here for my job, and for a new start. I do speak spanish. I learned both English and Spanish simultaneously."

The conversation flowed well between us. Twenty minutes turned into two hours. I felt so comfortable talking to him. I was on my second glass of wine, and it was like his voice was singing a tune that my pussy was reacting to. She had a mind of her own always, and I usually kept her locked away. Tonight, she was running the show. The words were out of my mouth before I could take them back.

"Can we skip the small talk and I come sit on your face?"

3

I was met with silence for about 3 seconds, Then, he said: *"Pull up."*

I'm playing Dirty by Tank hella loud on my way to him. I'm glancing at the GPS every 15 minutes or so. My hair is falling in my face because of the wind. When I get to a stoplight, I put my hair up in a bun. Thanks to this Rona mess, the bridge heading to him is basically deserted. I get there in record time. He's at the door with wet hair, and gray boxer briefs. His hair is either 3b or 3c. It's hard to tell in this light. It's a little past his shoulders, and thick. He smiles. Oh my. He has a gold and diamond grill at the bottom. I'm a Florida girl, and grills are my weakness. His eyes are brown, but in this light, they seem to sparkle. He has a nice beard that connects thank goodness. I think I'd just made a post about dudes whose beards don't connect. He moves to the side to let me in. He's taller than me, not that it matters at this point. It did bother me sometimes when men weren't taller than me. Being a tall girl with a short guy made me feel inadequate somehow, especially if they kept bringing it up all the time. My mouth forms an O looking around his place. It's nice. High ceilings. Dark blue and silver are the colors I see. Hardwood floors, with nice throw rugs. Paintings of real art are hanging up, mostly abstract pieces. Big arched long windows, with blue and silver curtains. They're not closed yet, and the view is breathtaking. You can see the ocean from here. The sunset is beautiful in the background. It looks like a painting almost. Leather sectional. Huge curved flat screen. Cute lil bar. I'm walking around slowly, and he hugs me from behind. Just like on the phone, he makes me feel safe, and comfortable. Like I've known him before. It's weird but it makes me tingle inside.

He kisses my neck, and I drop my keys and place my iPhone on his glass end table. he's still holding me from behind. Now he's licking my neck. I'm moaning softly. He starts pulling my clothes off and I'm silent, anticipating. Then before I can hold it in, I blurt out my thoughts.

"Please, I say."

"Please what."

"I need it."

He pulls his boxer briefs down.

"What do you need?"

He looks at me with this sexy ass smirk, while his dick just bounces against his thigh. He had the prettiest dick I've ever seen. Pretty light brown, oiled up, thick, manscaped, slightly curved, uncircumcised dick. My mouth goes dry. I want this deep down my throat.

"Please, I say again."

"What do you need?"

"Your dick in my mouth."

"Beg for it."

Oh we're doing this are we, I'm wondering. Fuck it, I'm here now. Let's do this.

"Please. Please Daniel."

I'm on my knees in front of him. Naked now. I take my hair out of the bun. My long plaits are caressing my back. My big DD nipples are standing at attention. My mouth is beginning to salivate. He walks over with his muscled hairy legs and this seductive walk. He feeds me the dick slowly. I'm greedy. I take it slowly, then I start gulping it. I'm guessing it's close to 7 inches, but it's the thickness that has my pussy getting wet. He pulls my braids away from my face. I'm looking up at him, and he's caressing my face.

"You're so fucking pretty. Look at you swallowing the dick. You love sucking this dick, don't you?"

"Fuck yes."

I'm choking on the dick, for his benefit mostly. I don't have a gag reflex. Men love to hear those choking noises. Spit is everywhere. I'm taking all of the dick in my mouth, and some down my throat. It's tickling my tonsils. My eyes and nose are running. I'm gagging and looking up at him moaning. He attempts to pull his dick away, but I won't let him.

"*Please. Please. I need it.*" I attempt to say with a mouthful of dick.

"*Tell me what you need.*"

"*Your cum. I want every drop. Please. Please Daniel.*"

He looks at me. He relaxes against me. I take that as a green light. I go into overdrive. I'm swallowing, choking, sucking and moaning. Saliva is dripping down on both breasts, and I pretend that this floor isn't bothering me, as I'm on my knees. His dick swells more and gets so hard in my mouth. My prize is soon to come, I just know it. I'm going all the way down his shaft. My soft lips are against his belly.

"*What the fuck? Damn girl.*"

I lick out my tongue, with my lips against his stomach, and saliva drips down his balls. He's shaking hard. I moan. It shoots out fast, thick and warm. I look up at him and swallow every drop. He helps me up off my knees, and I'm definitely grateful. I don't think I was gonna get up all cute after that. We're staring at each other. He puts his hands around my neck and pulls me close to him. He kisses me slow and deeply. His beard tickles my face a little. When we break away to catch our breath, he grabs my hand and leads me to his bed. I snatch up my cell phone. The lit candles lead the way. The sun has definitely gone down. A king size bed with a black upholstered wingback headboard and black silk sheets is up ahead. Candles are lit by the bed. Music is playing softly from some hidden speakers. It's so low that I can't make out the words. The beat is steady though. I know this song, I just can't place it yet.

"*Lay on your back and spread your legs.*"

"*Daniel?*"

"*Yes?*"

"*Can I record you?*"

He laughs uneasily. "*If it's gonna stay between us.*"

"I promise it'll be strictly for our collection. We'll both have a copy. That's if you feeling it."

"Fuck it, we made it this far."

I sit on the bed and scoot back to the middle. I grab my phone and tap the camera and make sure the flash is on. I lift my hair up so I'm not laying on it. I try to position myself at a good angle. I look up and he's watching me. He looks sexy as fuck. To see him in person, and in this light, he doesn't look like Clark Kent from Superman at all. He looks more like a darker version of Jason Momoa with a grill and a voice that's definitely hood. Fuck. He walks slowly to the bed, then hesitates, and reaches towards the bedside table. He grabs a ponytail holder and puts his hair up. He is so damn sexy. He pulls my legs a little bit, and I am closer to him. I watch him as he starts softly stroking my legs. He strokes my pussy softly.

"Your pussy fat af. How you get it so soft and hairless in a fucking pandemic?"

"I keep it waxed, and I exfoliate it every other day. Waxing lasts longer than shaving, and my girl does house calls."

"Pretty ass pussy."

He dips his head down, and I make sure I get him at a great angle. He is lapping my pussy up slowly like cream. He spreads my pussy lips softly and starts sucking my clit slowly.

"Damn you so sexy, with them sexy ass eyes. You know exactly how I need it. Eat that pussy Daniel."

He looks up at me and just moans. I feel a chill go over my body. My thighs are shaking uncontrollably on their own. He parts my legs and continues. He's eating my pussy like the taste is something he's been yearning for.

"This pussy taste so fucking good."

Just the words that I needed to hear. He moans and slides a finger inside me. I'm quivering and trying to keep the camera straight.

"You like the way I'm eating this pussy baby"?

"Yes I moan out. Fuck yes Daniel."

"This my damn pussy. I'm gonna make this pussy mine."

Why men do that? Don't ask questions, just stay in the moment sometimes. Before I can respond, he's sucking my clit faster, and I feel my body preparing for the release I need. The release I've been aching for. Fuck.

"Don't drop that phone, hold it steady. Capture me making you cum. I wanna watch that shit over and over."

I'm groaning and shaking and trying to hold it steady. The camera is on his face, his hair, his pretty ass fingers, with short clean fingernails, and pink ass tongue. I don't know if I can hold this phone and cum. It washes over me like a wave. My thighs clench, my clit swells, I start feeling sweat on my forehead, and I'm shaking like a leaf.

"Fuck. Please. Swallow all of it. Get all of it Daniel."

My body seizes, but I don't drop the phone. My cum starts rushing out of me, and he catches it. All of it. Every drop. The camera catches him looking up with a wet face perfectly. My wetness coats his face, and it's a beautiful sight. Dripping off his beard, shining and glistening in the candlelight. I'm so glad I'm capturing this on video. The piercing look in his eyes, when he stares at me, makes me give him my complete attention. It's breathtaking.

"I'm gonna fuck the shit out of you."

I lay back against the soft sheets, and I'm staring in his eyes as he comes over me. We have a moment of silence, where we're just staring at each other.

"Turn over."

I do exactly what he asks. I put my face in the sheets, spread my legs, and show him how pristine my arch is. I immediately start slowly rubbing my clit. I feel his tongue against my pussy again and I moan so loudly. I love every bit of this. He spreads my pussy lips and begins to tongue fuck my pussy from behind. I'm grinding slowly up against his face, moaning his name so loudly.

"Your pussy taste so damn good. Fuck."

He slurps and sucks me until I feel the bed getting wet.

"You ready for this dick?"

"Yes. Fuck yes."

He enters me slowly and I'm so grateful. I'm used to average and small dicks, and his pretty ass dick is something I need to adjust to. He's so thick, I feel my pussy stretching to accommodate him. I inhale slowly and exhale even slower. He knows this is an adjustment. He's taking mercy on me and I appreciate it. He slowly fills my pussy up with his thick uncircumcised dick.

"You ok? Tell me. I'm not hurting you, am I?"

"Daniel please don't stop."

He's moving his hips slowly, like he's hearing a beat or feeling it. It's almost like he's in sync with the song playing in the background. In and out he strokes me. He pulls his dick all the way out, and slowly slams it back deep inside me. I wanna scream, but I settle for grabbing a pillow and putting my face in it. I'm moaning, groaning, and my body has submitted completely to him, and he has no idea. I'm definitely not going to tell him. He's groaning and moving so smoothly. He grabs my hair, wraps it around his hand, and pulls me back against him. He kisses me sloppily. I'm moaning into his mouth, and he loves it.

"Please Daniel don't stop. Fuck me. Stop this fucking ache."

"That's what you need huh, to be fucked hard?"

"Yes please, please."

He pushes my face back into the bed, and I arch even more to give him the best access. He seemingly goes into overdrive. He starts fucking me so hard, his pelvis is slamming into me. Clapping sounds is all you hear.

"Don't stop. Please don't stop. Fuck me!"

His dick is so hard, and I'm so wet, I'm dripping down my thighs. I'm still rubbing my clit slow. I hear him making a sucking sound. I glance back at him, and he's sucking on his finger. I watch him as He takes that wet index finger and sticks it slowly inside my asshole. I pause because I'm not used to this. I stop breathing for a second. But after a little bit, it feels so good. I'm throwing my pussy and ass back against him. He's catching it and matching me thrust for thrust. I'm shaking and lost in my desire. I don't want this feeling to end. Damn I really hadn't been fucked right in a long ass time.

"Cum on this dick. Cum for me." He slaps my ass hard twice.

Him saying those words is all I needed. My orgasm overwhelms me. I feel my pussy muscles clenching his thick dick. It feels like I'm trying to push his dick out of me. I keep having spasms and jerking against him. I cum twice. He's still hard, and I'm wondering if he's a machine, or if he took something before I got here. I look up at him in amazement.

"Oh, baby you in for a treat. It always takes me awhile to get that 2nd nut. Ride this dick."

In my mind I'm thinking ride? Nigga I'm drained already. But then this has been an experience, and who knows when I'll be able to get quarantine dick again. Fuck it. He lays on his back and scoots back up against his huge headboard.

"Come on, I'm gonna help you ride this dick."

All I'm thinking is thank goodness. I move over to him, and get on my knees, and prepare to straddle him.

"No, baby sit all the way down on it. Squat on the dick and stay on your toes."

So, he wants me to ride ride today? I better cum at least twice more. I hover over him, and squat down on his dick slowly. As soon as he's inside me, my pussy is struggling to adjust. Taking him this way is harder. He's deep inside me, stretching me. I'm breathing hard, and he clasps my hands tight, and we both get used to this position. He lets my hands go and starts stroking my back and ass.

"Fuck me."

I'm on my toes riding him slowly and getting used to this dick. When I go all the way down, I squeeze my pussy tightly, and when I'm about halfway up it, I squeeze it again. His eyes roll back, and he squeezes my ass so hard, that I know he likes it. His head is against the headboard, and I take one hand and put it around his neck and squeeze. He looks up at me and says nothing, he just watches me. There's the look again. His eyes are so damn sexy.

"You like that?"

"Fuck yes I do. You keep this up and I'm gonna cum."

A part of me is like thank goodness. This riding is a fucking workout. I've got a rhythm going now. I'm swirling my hips, I'm rocking, and I'm squeezing my pussy on his dick. This is the workout I've needed this entire quarantine, so I guess I won't complain. I'm gonna be sore as fuck tomorrow. I look down at him and I smirk. I put my hands on the bed, and I stop moving for a few seconds.

"Babe, what are you doing?"

I don't answer him. I spin around so that I'm facing his feet. I don't take his dick out at all.

"Damn, what the fuck?"

In this reverse cowgirl position, I can really go hard. It feels so much better this way, especially with his thick curved dick. It's hitting every spot so perfectly. I'm zoning out, and I had no idea I would be feeling like this. I'm still on my feet riding the hell out of his dick. I look over and see a mirror, and I see myself riding his dick. The darkness and candlelight has me looking good on top of him. I'm turning myself on more. I'm rubbing my left breast with one hand and alternating with the other breast. He starts fingering my ass as I continue in this reverse cowgirl position. When I take him deep on that downward stroke, I do a swirl and body roll on his dick. I can tell he likes this. I see his toes curling up.

"Yes, make me nut again."

I take that as a challenge. I let go of my breasts. I'm rubbing my clit faster now. I wanna cum when he does. His finger is putting in work in my ass. I'm not sure if I wanna try anal, but this finger feels good. My legs feel like they're about to give up. It's almost like we're talking telepathically. He takes his free hand and starts helping me ride him. He takes his finger out of my ass, and I actually miss it. He has both hands on my hips and is guiding me to ride him faster. I'm fucking him and moaning his name loudly. He's moaning and saying *"Fuck"* every other word. I feel his dick expanding and throbbing inside me, and I increase my clit stimulation. I tell him I'm about to cum.

"Yes baby, cum all over this dick. Wet ass good ass pussy. Cum on that fucking dick."

As soon as I feel my body lock up, I feel him tilting his hips up, and fucking me fast. He grabs me close, and I feel him breathing against me hard. He holds me tightly as he cums. I can't lie, I don't want this moment to end. After a few minutes, we've caught our breath, and I try to get up off his dick, but my legs are wobbly. He sees my dilemma and helps me off him. We're side by side, and we're facing each other.

"Can you spend the night?"

"Do you want me to?

"I don't want you to leave."

"I'll stay as long as you want me to."

He looks in my eyes and kisses my forehead.

"I'm gonna make you mine."

Chapter 2

THE COMEDY SHOW

I hadn't been out of the house in months. The kids were at my moms and I had the weekend all to myself. The comedy show wasn't for a few hours. I was in bed turned on, needing relief, but not sure if I should just ignore it or use my vibrator right quick. I looked at the time. Almost 4 hours until showtime. Fuck it. I reached in my nightstand drawer, and grabbed my favorite vibrator, a high-powered bullet. I opened my laptop and navigated to one of my favorite porn sites. After a few minutes of previewing a few clips, I settled on this threesome with two women and a man. It wasn't your normal threesome. The man was submissive, and the women were very much dominant. They were giving him orders, taking turns choking and riding him, while he complied to their commands. One was making him eat her pussy while the other girl was eating his ass then she starts pegging him and he's so into it. It took less than five minutes of me watching and my pussy was clenching, and I was shaking and breathing hard. I definitely wanted more, but it would take too long to cum again and I was pressed for time. I put my toy up after I cleaned it, closed my laptop and headed to the shower. This was a well needed escape from reality. I had been single for 5 years, after a messy divorce. It took me 3 years to get over him, and actually cut my soul ties from him. The healing part was a transition, but I'm grateful that I learned so much. I was grateful that I was me again finally. I know some of y'all can relate. I had been sporadically dating this last year and a half but hadn't met anyone special or felt that any of them had potential. It had been months since I went on a real date, and I hadn't had sex with anyone in a year.

All I wanted tonight was to enjoy myself and step out of my little box. Lately, I'd been going places alone and it was definitely freeing. I loved it. I was very careful though, and I was always carrying my gun and pepper spray with me. You could never be too prepared. I was heavy on vibes too. If something or someone didn't feel right, I got the hell away. I never second guessed myself. I always trusted my instincts.

Anyway, I was so excited about tonight, and going to this comedy show. I loved to laugh. I usually chose small venues and hadn't been to a comedy show this big since I left my ex-husband. Tonight, was going to be a special night, I could just feel it. All the necessary prerequisites were done. Hair, nails, facial, massage and shopping of course. I'd been preparing all week. I elected to wear one of my heels from my closet. Not to say that I didn't purchase more pairs of shoes, I just wasn't choosing to wear those tonight. I was a shoe fanatic, and I didn't go shopping without buying at least one pair. I didn't want the night spent breaking new heels in.

I'd seen advertisements for a while about this show all over social media. The closer it came to the actual show date, the more it was talked about. It was headlined by Mike Epps and included some other hilarious talents as well. I rarely listened to the radio, but one day while sitting in traffic, scanning my playlist for the right song, I heard them say that there were still tickets at the door. I didn't trust that at all. I'd hate to show up just to be told it was sold out. That's what ultimately led me to purchase my ticket online right then and there. It was definitely gonna be in the nose bleeds, but at this late in the game, I wasn't going to complain. I got in my dark blue colored Acura SUV, and was greeted by Hussle and Motivate by Nipsey Hussle when the car started, blasting out of my speakers. He was one of my go to rappers to get me in the right frame of mind, to get ready for work and face the day. Him and Tupac provided my motivation so to speak. I didn't want to get hyped or motivated right now. Tonight, I needed something more mellow and calm. I scanned through my playlist, until I found the perfect song. Jhene Aiko it is. Wasted love started playing as I hit reverse. Her voice was always so soothing and relaxing. Healing actually. It definitely was putting me in the mood I needed to be in. I was usually a stickler for punctuality, so I left the house extra early, trying to account for traffic. I was glad I did. I was making good time and the Tampa traffic was flowing smoothly. The first 20 miles in was a breeze. When I was maybe 5 miles away from the arena, the Tampa traffic started to slow, and brake lights could be seen flashing in every lane. The once smooth flowing traffic was now at a crawl. I wasn't going to complain at all. That's why you prepare. At least the traffic was still moving, even if it was slow as snails.

    I took this time to look in the mirror at myself. I'm not a big makeup girl, but I had a light face beat tonight. A very natural look that accentuated my almond shaped eyes and high cheekbones. I had my air on full blast. It was way too humid in Florida to have my windows down. I usually loved wavy hair, but tonight I was rocking Brazilian mink straight hair in black, with a frontal that had me asking what lace. I had on a cute little olive dress that was form fitting with a split coming up my left thigh. I found it online from a black owned boutique. The dress was very classy to me. Short sleeved, and lightweight. Not too tight, and it was stretchable. It was a dress you could dress up or down. I'd chosen to dress it up a little. My cute beige ankle strap Giuseppe heels had me looking and feeling so sexy tonight. My earrings were diamond studs that I'd had for years. My lips were glossy, and my d cups were sitting at attention thanks to this cute bra from SavageFenty. This olive green against my peanut butter skin tone was definitely a great choice. Ever since I'd found myself again, fell madly in love with me, and started working out I loved what I saw in the mirror every day. I was changing the way I thought about things too. I was trying to be more optimistic and positive. I had started changing my attitude and my reactions to certain situations. Glass half full and all that.

Twenty minutes later, I was walking in the building, shoulder to shoulder with the crowd. I'm a tall girl, about 6'2" with these heels on and 5'9" barefoot. Dangerous curves on a stallion. This was a very mixed crowd. Mixed as in different shades of brown skin. The couple Caucasian people I happened upon were few and far between. I found the area where I was sitting pretty easily, after glancing at my tickets a few times, to make sure I was right. I saw a bar not far from the double doors serving drinks. I ordered a rum and coke and set off to climb those stairs. The seats next to mine were empty for now and when I checked my phone, it showed that I still had 30 minutes before the show started. I sat in my seat, began scrolling social media, Twitter and IG mostly, and languidly sipped my drink. It disappeared in no time, in spite of the slow sips, and I wasn't feeling the least bit buzzed. I needed more liquor and less chaser. I went back downstairs for another round. I asked the bartender to make it a double this time. She had to be at most 5'3". She had on a blonde lace front wig, that actually accentuated her dark skin. She was quite beautiful. The kind of beautiful that you get distracted by. At first glance she reminded me of Jill Marie Jones, aka Toni Childs, from the hit tv show girlfriends. Same lips, but different nose, with these piercing light brown eyes. When she handed me my drink, she smiled, and I made sure to tip her well. We black women have to look out for each other. I definitely wanted to enjoy my night.

The music was blasting from the stage by the time I'd made it back through the double doors so I knew it wouldn't be long now before they would begin. I was swaying along with the beat, feeling the alcohol just a bit now. As I headed up the stairs to my seat, I looked up to see a dark skin bald dude with a fantastic beard. It was glowing like he was using a good brand of beard products. His skin glistened. Not in a maybe he put baby oil on it but more of a well taken care of skin glow. Someone who exfoliates and spends a little extra on creams, oils and facials. He's dark like Djimon Honsu, and I love it. He reminds me of dark chocolate, and I wanna know if it's slightly bitter, or sweet. I could lick the top of his bald head right now. I smile to myself at my wayward thoughts. I always pay close attention to details. Sitting beside me, his thighs are thicker and longer than mine. He's definitely tall, and he definitely works out. He looks at me, and I look at him. We both share an easy smile. His eyes are a lighter brown than mine. In contrast to his skin, they are quite striking and captivating. In my mind, I'm thinking that he has to be here with someone, he's gotta be married, or at the least in a relationship. The good ones usually are. But who knows if he's a good one? I could smell him before I even got settled in my seat good. Definitely expensive cologne but subtle, not allergy or sinus inducing at all. Nice.

"How are you this evening?"

His eyes are definitely flirting with me. I'm definitely not imagining that, or am I?

"I'm good, how are you?"

"I'm Kevin, and you are?"

I tell him my friends call me Storm. I wasn't eager to give him my real name. Serial killers aren't usually God awful to look at. They aren't usually black or Latino either, but I'll digress on that. We engage in idle chitchat and we both reveal that we're here alone. By this time, I start to feel a heartbeat starting deep inside my pussy. A steady beat like a great Freddie Gibbs rap record. I'm fidgeting in my seat. Squirming actually. I'm definitely getting turned on but trying not to make it obvious. At that precise moment of course, he asks if I'm uncomfortable and I have to laugh it off. No way I could just say that I'm getting turned on by him. No way I could tell him that my mouth was watering, thinking of what his cum would taste like. You don't say those types of things to a complete stranger. Or at least I never had. I was feeling bold tonight, but not that bold.

The show starts and I promise I'm trying to ignore him. That seems like the smart thing to do. I do peep that he isn't wearing a wedding ring. But in this day and age, that really means nothing. It could be in his pocket for Pete's sake. He's drinking some brown liquor with no chaser, just ice. When he smiles, his white teeth shine so brightly. Be still my heart, or my pussy, is what I'm thinking, but I can't tell which one at this point. As the show progresses, the alcohol starts leaving an effect on us both and it seems we've inadvertently gotten closer to each other. A particular joke is funny to us both, and he lightly touches my thigh, and at other times, I'm touching his shoulder. His breath smells of mint wintergreen and cognac. Mmm, that's what was in his cup. Mine probably mirrors his. Our eyes meet and held for a few seconds longer than they should have. I'm having a full-blown conversation with myself in my head. I'm like, Ok, is he feeling what I'm feeling right now? This energy is crazy. I bite my lip and try to stay focused on the show. I laugh when the crowd laughs, but I can't even tell you what the joke is. How can I? This man is intoxicating, and the energy between us seems to have ignited. Like you can feel it in the air. I'm having filthy thoughts about him, shamelessly. Yes, it most definitely has been awhile.

My earlier use of my toy didn't stop this ache I had. I bite my bottom lip, in hopes of it breaking me out of these inappropriate thoughts. His thighs make me wanna straddle him. I always felt that way around men taller than me. I want to kiss him until I'm out of breath. I want him fucking me deep and pulling my hair. When he looks in my eyes it's almost like he's capturing my soul. How could that be? I'm so wet, I feel it gushing slowly out of my pussy and down the inside of my thighs. This is the reason why I should have worn panties. I rarely ever go out in public without them. Yet for some reason, tonight I had to forego normalcy. But a tight dress doesn't hit as well with panty lines. Definitely should have at least put on a thong. But my ass was sitting so right in this dress. Thongs have always been so uncomfortable for me. Anything purposely up my butt, wasn't ever going to be enjoyable. Well, at least not panties. I didn't want panty lines showing or anything else distracting from my curves. I didn't plan on coming out and being turned on either. At least not this early. I hadn't been here long. Lord knows I rain or storm when I get wet. Hence the nickname Storm, given to me by an ex-lover.

Earthquake is finishing his set, and I slip away to the bathroom. I'm counting each step, willing myself not to fall. I'm trying to walk all cute to this bathroom. It was actually a brisk walk. Half because of the liquor, and needing to relieve myself, and the other half is me needing to clean up my thighs and wipe away this moisture from my pussy. I don't need to wet this dress up. Sommore is walking onstage as I slip down the steps finally. Most people are rooted to their seats because Mike Epps is up next. There's no line at the women's restroom and I hurry right in. I'm in a handicap stall so I have the sink in front of me while I clean this wetness off, praying it's not on my dress. I use the toilet quickly, then I set about the task of cleaning myself up. Thank goodness I brought some wipes in my purse. My dress is up at my waist bunched up, and I'm hoping it doesn't get wrinkled. I hadn't been cleaning up for a full minute, and someone knocks on the door.

"Just a minute", I yell out.

I'm pulling my dress down, and I'm thinking this person must really be handicap. My face is probably beet red with embarrassment. I decide to wash my hands at the outer sinks, to allow this person use of this stall. I open the door, see men's clothes and I look up, and it's him. Our eyes lock, and this time neither one of us looks away. The reason I'm even in here with an overflowing pussy is him. My face is one of shock, curiosity and honestly need.

"What are you doing in here?"

"I needed to see you. I needed to know if you were alright."

Then he smirks.

"I also wanted to know if you were as turned on as I am."

Well damn. Definitely not going according to my plan. My mouth goes dry, and it takes a few seconds for me to respond.

"What makes you think I'm turned on?"

I reply coyly. knowing damn well I wanna swallow all his cum at this point.

"I wasn't sure. But I wanted to taste you and see for myself."

There's my mouth, going dry again. Damn. There my pussy goes, gushing again. I shake my head.

"You don't even know my real name."

"So, Storm wasn't your real name? I had no idea."

He smirks after his sarcastic reply. I bite my lips and I can't stay still. I do that when I'm turned on.

"Kevin is actually my name baby girl. So, you wanna give me an alias? Cool. But does it really matter though? We are two consenting adults with adult needs. No rules, no worries, just this moment right now."

"You say that like you're married. You probably are. Just my fucking luck. Yet another married man that wants to fuck me. Great."

I roll my eyes fast.

"I assure you that I'm not married. I want to do more than just fuck you, but I figured with your permission, you should let me taste you first. If you have any questions, I'd love to answer them. But I also figured that since I'm in the women's restroom, you'd want to question me later, before someone walks in, and allow me to do what I've been thinking of, since you sat down beside me. Tasting your pussy."

Fuck. I loved his honesty and bravado. This handsome specimen wanted to taste my pussy. I wondered if he was any good at it, and if he could actually make me cum. Fuck it, let's find out. I'm gonna let him taste my pussy, in the women's restroom at a comedy show. What are the odds? I back up until my ass is against the oversized sink. I look in his eyes and I realize that we're really about to do this. He comes in the stall and locks the door behind him. I pull my dress up again. He licks his lips.

"Yes baby. Look at that pretty pussy. I knew it would be just as pretty as you. Completely bare except for that cute lil triangle and no panties. I like. I like this very much. Look at her glistening. So, you were turned on?"

I bite my bottom lip and blush. He gets on his knees and looks up at me.

"Spread those pretty pussy lips for me."

I oblige him. I spread my pussy open for him and feel exposed to the world. Yet in that moment, I don't care. He starts off licking all over my pussy. She's so slippery that it's hard to keep her open. He sucks softly on my clit.

"Look at that pretty ass clit. It's like a rosebud. Pretty as fuck."

I moan and get closer to his face. He sucks and licks, swallows, and sucks some more. He's moaning as he buries his tongue inside me, and I start rubbing my clit slowly.

"Please don't stop."

He looks up at me.

"I don't intend to. You will cum before I stop, and only then if you tell me to."

Our eyes meet. I throw my head back as he continues. He places one finger, then tries two inside me, and puts his tongue on my clit again. He's licking it and sucking it. He pushes my skin up some so my clit is more exposed. He is so experienced. He knows exactly what he is doing. I've been looking for a man like this forever. An award winner of the pussy eaters. I'm rubbing his shiny head and moaning. Making him get closer to this pussy, literally riding his face. He's a tall man, so on his knees, he's the perfect height for me to stand and ride his face to my enjoyment. He delights in me getting off the edge of the sink and riding his face like a seat. He's moaning and grunting and inhaling my scent. I could explode any minute now. I love when a man enjoys eating pussy. This is erotic as fuck.

"Mmhmm. Yes. This pussy taste so damn good", he says between lip smacks. "Ride my face, wet it up, soak this fucking beard. Do it."

I get chills all over my body. My heart is racing and I'm soaking wet. That definitely propels me to act up. I'm holding his head, as I ride his face. I look down at him, as I'm holding his head in the perfect position.

"You want me to wet up your fucking face huh. Mmmhmmm. Don't stop. Keep working those fingers and that tongue. God."

I'm breathing faster, and I'm riding his face, and I have no regard for if he's comfortable like this or not. I'm totally concentrating on exploding on his face. I know that's exactly what he wants. Oh God. Oh fuck. I'm feeling my body tighten like a spring. My legs began to shake, and my toes are scrunched up in my heels. I tell him that I'm about to cum, and he takes that to mean go harder. He sucks on my clit for dear life and his fingers are in overdrive.

"Cum for me baby."

I look down at him looking up at me as he says that, and that's all it takes. It's something about a deep demanding voice. I shake and jerk and I gush over his fingers, and onto his face. He's trying to catch as much of it as he can. Seeing my cum on his face is the most beautiful thing. Coating his beard with my release makes me wish I could have recorded this. I'm bold bold tonight. I sigh deeply once I'm able to articulate my thoughts. At that exact moment, a few women have come into the restroom, laughing and giggling amongst themselves. I put my fingers to my lips, which smell so fucking good, with my scent all over them. I telepathically try to convey to him that he isn't to make a sound. Especially with that deep voice. It would definitely rat us out. I pull my dress down, and head to the sink. I put the hot water on, grab a few wipes from my purse, and soap them up and hand them to him. Usually, I clean my partner up after anything sexual, but there's no time and he's technically not my partner. He's soaping up his face and once again I'm cleaning my thighs and pussy. We both try to stifle our laughs until they leave. When the coast is clear, we both laugh and I fall against him, touch his chest with my hand, and look up at him. He smiles at me and kisses my forehead. I melt inside but try to keep a straight face. Forehead kisses for me hit different. I walk out ahead of him once we're done, wanting to make sure no one sees him. Thinking back on it, that really wouldn't have worked anyway since he's so much taller than me. Next time we should go to the men's restroom. He'd definitely be able to hide me being behind him. Wait, did I just say next time? We make it back to our seats and the show is still going. My face was red from feeling embarrassed, thinking that everyone knows what we just did.

Of course, they don't have a clue. After a minute or so, I visually relax, and give my full attention to Mike Epps.

By the end, we're both clapping and agreeing how good the show was. We decide to stay in our seats, when it's time to go. I hate getting caught in crowds. People are stampeding to the exit, while he and I watch them and make small talk, like the scent of my pussy isn't still on his breath and his face. After about 15 minutes, the crowd has mostly dispersed, and we make our way down the steps.

He touches my arm, before I turn the corner, and I stop, and look up at him.

"Well pretty lady, there is so much more that I want to do to you, if you'll allow me."

I look up at him with a blank stare.

"I have a hotel room a few miles away. The Hilton Suites, Room 317. No pressure but I'd love for you to join me. We could have a nightcap and do whatever you're comfortable doing. What do you say?"

I'm at a loss for words and my overthinking is in overdrive. He saves the moment thankfully.

"I'll tell you what, don't even answer, I'll be there waiting. If you

show up, I'll take that as confirmation that you want more from me tonight. If you don't show, at least we will both have the memory of what transpired here not long ago."

He leans over, kisses my forehead again and walks away, with his scent permeating my clothes, and the smell of my pussy on his face. Fuck. He's so sexy and handsome. He's definitely running game, but he is intriguing to me. Intriguing usually meant dangerous, but in any case, I didn't even care.

That was a smooth walk away he did, I definitely gotta hand that to him. Even his walk was sexy. It reminded me of Morris Chestnut in The Best Man, the scene when he's walking away because he knows Harper slept with Mia. I still was indecisive and stood there for a few minutes, trying to get the nerve to leave. Wondering if I was really going to fuck a complete stranger. Knowing that I knew the answer already. I was just lying to myself for the moment. Stalling, trying to just experience this and not overthink everything. To stay in the moment and feel all of this. But hell, I was grown, and I needed this. I deserved this.

My pussy needed this and so did my heart. Where did that come from? These damn Cancer emotions were all over the place all the damn time. Whatever. I pushed that thought to the back of my mind.

GPS showed that he really was right down the road. I pulled up at the Hilton less than fifteen minutes later and gave the valet up front my keys. When I got close to the elevator, I decided to make a quick restroom trip to make sure I wasn't looking disheveled plus my nerves were bad. I was shaking. I remembered that I had a shot of Dusse left in my flask in my purse. I was nothing if not prepared. I quickly down the rest of the shot. I immediately relax. I do a quick hair fluff and a side to side turn. I pop a couple mints in my mouth and start sucking on them hard. I look in the mirror with a little smirk and head to the elevator. 10 minutes later I was at his door. I felt a little nervous, but the alcohol had me ignoring it or maybe I was full of bravado tonight. Perhaps both. He opened the door, and just stared at me. He literally looked me up and down as if he was trying to decide which part of me to taste first. I was so giddy inside.

"Hi."

"Hi. Come in."

The room was nice. The view was a cute vibe. The bathroom was beautiful. Clear shower with big double shower heads. A nice egg-shaped oversized tub, sat in the middle of the bathroom that automatically gave me thoughts on what we could do in it. The room smelled of him. The top three buttons of his shirt were unbuttoned, and his sleeves were rolled up. God, I wished this man was mine. I had no idea why that thought went through my mind. Yet deep down, my heart did. I was not going to let my emotions ruin this night for me. I shut a lid on these Cancer feelings quick. No overthinking tonight. This was just sex. I smiled at him.

"I have a request," he said, smiling down at me.

"Can we pretend that we actually belong to each other for the next 24 hours?"

I definitely needed to find out what his sign was. I was momentarily stupefied. Definitely at a loss for words. What was he, a mind reader? Some sort of psychic? And he said the next 24 hours, not the next few hours. He wanted to spend that much time with me?

It didn't even matter at this point, I was willing to take what he'd give.

"I'd like that."

"How do you feel about getting in that tub with me? We can put your hair up, if you need to. I know how women are about their hair."

"I can clip it up."

I went looking through my overnight bag and found the clip. I'm always prepared with an overnight bag. You just never knew when you'll need it and a single gal like myself must stayed prepared. Most would call it a hoe bag, but I hadn't had sex in a year, so that assumption is way off, or was it? He started the water. He began taking his clothes off and I did the same. We stood there staring at each other naked for a little bit. Brother must never miss gym days. His chest and back are wide in contrast to his waist. It all looks like a perfect V. His abs are nice, but you can tell that he still eats well if you know what I mean.

He definitely had the body type I prefer on a man. Thick. His skin was the color of Hershey's chocolate. His nipples were even darker. I want to run my tongue across his nipples. Nice short nails with no polish. A birthmark on his side that reminded me of a jelly fish. Those nice muscular legs proved he never skipped leg day at the gym either. His dick is so thick. It's not huge, but it's a bit longer than average, and definitely thicker than most. Circumcised with a slight curve to the left. He was walking perfection to me. Soft curly hair on his chest and lower stomach that just made me want to get on my knees and inhale his scent. He put his hands in the water to test the temperature.

"Feels good. Try it out."

I put my hands in the water as well and it felt perfect. I put my white gel painted toenails in first, getting in slowly. I sink into the water and visibly relax. It stung a little against my back but it felt good after a few seconds. I'm scooting my back to the back of the tub when he touches me gently on my shoulder.

"I want to be behind you."

I scoot forward and let him get in. This tub was the perfect size for the both of us. I needed this at home. Once he's adjusted to his comfort, I scoot back against him and lay the back of my head against his chest. It felt so good and so familiar like we'd been doing this for years. It was almost like we knew each other before tonight. I felt comfortable with him. I loved our energy together.

He begins to rub my shoulders and I totally relax against him then. We stay that way for a few minutes. He kisses my shoulders and tells me he wants to make love to me. I can feel him getting hard behind me. I turn to face him and kiss his soft lips. I kiss him slowly and deeply and he accepts my tongue, sucking on it. I give him my answer without saying a word. We separate momentarily to catch our breath. He lathers up a washcloth and washes my back and neck. I can't remember the last time a man did this for me. He washes me all over and I am shaking with need, wanting him, needing him. I go to wash him and he stops my hand.

"Tonight is all about you. I want you to go Lay on the bed with your legs spread wide. Take the clip out of your hair and wait there just like that for me."

This is like a dream that I don't want to wake from. I've always felt like I was a giver in relationships, or hell situationships. I have gone out of my way to make sure every partner of mine was satisfied. Drained even. To be on the receiving end is exactly what I've deserved. This may only be lasting one night, but I was going to savor this for as long as I could.

I pat myself dry, and head over to the bed. I'm aware that his eyes are watching me intently. It makes me feel so sexy. Desired. Needed. I'm having thoughts of his bald head between my legs. Just thinking of it makes me moan. Before I realize it, my imagination has become a reality. I feel his lips against my fingers, soft kisses on each one. I open my legs wide, and part the lips of my pussy. I feel nothing but the coolness of the air in the room, and not the heat of him, so I sit up slightly. He's at the end of the bed. My mouth goes dry just looking at him. He looks at me and I stare back at him.

"Prop up on a pillow. I want you to watch me. I want you to see everything."

I do just as he says. Once situated, I resume opening my pussy for him. He approaches like a tiger, slowly. Anticipating, needing. He swirls his tongue, he sucks, and he licks. He moans as he tastes me. I'm getting more turned on by the second. He puts his finger inside of me and continues focusing on my clit.

I'm slowly rubbing his head, attempting to savor every moment. I scoot down a little, and tilt towards his face, giving him better access to my pussy. He adds another finger, and then starts slowly pulling them out and putting them back in. He does a few come hither motions with his fingers, and I feel my body start to respond to him. It washes over me like a wave, and I start to tighten like a coil.

I lay my head back, and gaze up at the ceiling, with my mouth slightly agape.

"Please don't stop. I'm about to cum."

He pulls away and I look at him, wondering what he's planning and why he's stopping.

"No. Watch me. I wanna see your face as you cum. Alright?"

"Yes, Please just don't stop."

I make sure I'm focused on him as he resumes tasting and inhaling me.

"Fuck. Kevin please."

That sends him into overdrive. His fingers speed up, and the pressure from his mouth on my clit is increased. I feel my orgasm building and building. I let go of my pussy lips that are super slippery and I grip his head and hold it steady. I make sure I keep my focus on him. I do not turn away.

"Yes. Yes. Oh God yes."

I shake and I groan, and I cream on his tongue and his beard. I yell out his name over and over. I feel completely weakened, and very much satisfied. I bask in that realization for a while. I hadn't cum like this, from a man in years. He probably wouldn't believe that. Most didn't, but it was true. After a few seconds, I remind myself that I need to return the favor. I sit up slowly from my position in the bed. I look at him and notice that he's already been looking my way.

Without saying a word, I move close to him and take his hard dick in my hand. I examine it like it's a work of art. My mouth begins to water. It's so dark and beautiful. Perfect. He has enough length for me, but it's the girth and the slight curve, that makes me wanna know how this is going to feel deep inside me. I'm figuring that he's going to give me the stretching of a lifetime. I don't know if he's planning to take it easy on me or not but a part of me doesn't want him to. I want him to punish me with this dick. It's been so long since I've had any good dick. Hell, any dick period. I so needed this. Then I put it in my mouth and I moan like it's savory because it is. That clear precum has me wanting to guzzle every drop of him. I want to show him that I can please him just as well as he can please me. I push him against the headboard. He adjusts his pillow so he can really watch me. I enjoy being watched. I lay between his legs and take his dick in my hands. I make sure I look at him as I lick, suck, slurp, spit, and take as much of it as I can in this position. I neglect nothing. His balls, the gooch, everything I can put my tongue on or in. I'm moaning because I'm enjoying myself and he's starting to moan and that really turns me on. I kick it up a notch. I smirk inside like "oh you think that was all I had?" Bless your heart. As soon as I'm about to make him tap out, he stops me.

"I don't want to cum this way baby, at least not yet. I wanna make love to you too."

Damn it. I wanted that fucking cum. I have to have it. This is what I'm thinking at the moment. However, I don't want to let the cat all the way out the bag on our first night. But then again, I may never see him again. So, fuck it.

"Why can't you do both? Can you do both? I need your cum, I wanna swallow it. Please Kevin. I need it."

I look him in his eyes, and I don't look away.

He gets this look in his eyes that I don't need to hear the words to. Mmhmm. Precisely. I go to work. I continue sucking, slurping, moaning, jacking his dick, spitting on it, making vacuum like noises that men seem to appreciate, and my pussy gets wetter and wetter. He does this groan and I know I'll have my prize soon. His dick has gotten even harder in my mouth. A few seconds later I have a mouthful. A little salty with a smidgen of sweetness. It's yummy. I look him in his eyes, and I swallow every drop. I softly suck him a little more until he tells me it's too sensitive, and he can't take anymore. I back off and lay against the sheets. I am smiling like the Cheshire Cat on the inside.

"It's not over, it's only just begun."

I'm elated that he has more to give. I love that. I'm not used to that, not with men my age but it's something I've always dreamed of.

"Come ride my face. Bring that pretty pussy over here."

Fuck. He really is giving me the best night of my life.

He lays on his back, as I climb up his body. He makes sure I'm positioned just so.

"Open my pussy.

Fuck. I love hearing him say those words.

"Yes, your pussy."

I do exactly as he asks, but in my head, I'm thinking that I wish this was his pussy. All he needed to do was say the word.

I look down at the passion in his eyes. I'm so turned on. I want to savor every little moment, and not miss a thing. He pulls me closer to his mouth. I open his pussy wide. He devours me. The slurping and suction noises he is making is heightening the experience. I literally began to ride his face. Way better than I did in the handicap stall. I was free to really show out now. I close my eyes and I'm telling him not to stop. It's like I'm riding his face to a beat you can't hear. Then I pop my eyes back open when I remember that he wants me to watch. He goes back and forth from my clit to tongue fucking my pussy. Looking up at me with this sexy hungry look in his eyes like his appetite is insatiable and intoxicated by my scent. He's gripping my ass and smacks it as I ride him. I'm biting my lips to keep from screaming out loud.

"Wet my fucking face up. Don't you hold back a drop. Not this time. Give it all to me."

Fuck. I love how he talks to me.

His tongue is lapping up my juices and spearing my pussy so perfectly. I forget all about holding my pussy open for him. I've let go and I'm feeling my body tingle all over. I'm luxuriating in watching him eat my pussy like no other man has. Is tonight even real? I'm throwing my head back and my hair brushes my back like a whisper against my skin. It's so erotic.

"Don't stop. Please don't stop. Stay there, right where you are. Fuck. Don't you move. I want you to swallow all my cum."

He makes a moan of agreement and smacks my ass hard. That was all I needed to send me over the edge. I throw my head back even further and my body explodes. I feel myself gushing everywhere. I don't even have the energy to watch him swallow my nectar. My legs are now shaking like a stripper's ass. He helps me get untangled and off his face as I remember that he does need to breathe. In that moment he didn't seem to care. I am now on my back, eyes closed, still feeling aftershocks. Shaking, trembling and sensitive. I feel him get off the bed, and all I can do is whimper my disapproval. I hear him tearing open a foil packet and I'm smiling on the inside. I'm so ready to feel him deep inside me.

"I really wanna feel all of you. Do you want me to wear this?"

I look at him, and I shake my head. We'd both swallowed it all, why think of protection now, right? Perhaps I'd regret that tomorrow, but today, I didn't care. I want to feel his dick deep inside me. I want him to feel every clench of this pussy. A few seconds later, I get what I need. As he slowly puts the tip in, I feel my pussy trying to accommodate him. I haven't experienced a dick this wide in my whole life. He pushes in more, and I inhale deeply. I try to relax and think to myself that another shot would have been nice right now. Like a mind reader, he looks at me and smirks.

"Don't worry, I'm gonna take my time. I'm gonna take it easy on my pussy this time."

I visibly relax at those words. He's looking in my eyes and he pushes halfway inside of me. I go to gasp but he catches me for a kiss. A slow wet kiss. He talks to me as he's literally impaling me with his dick.

"I've been thinking of this all night. Your pussy so fucking wet and tight, damn the way you gripping this dick. How your pussy get so wet? It's wetter than it was at the concert. Wet tight ass pussy. You've been needing to get you some dick. Come here, come closer. Bring me this pussy. Get you some more of this dick. Imma give you all of this dick. Tight ass pussy. I'm gonna make love to this fat pussy, damn this really needs to be my fucking pussy."

He stops moving and looks down at me.

"Damn. I've never said this shit before, and actually meant it."

My insecurities and overthinking were about to rear their ugly head, so I smile up at him. I don't know if he's just gassing me up or if he means it. I don't want to analyze it right now. I don't even know if it matters.

So, I took this pause to my advantage.

"Let me ride this dick. My dick for the night."

"Shit girl, your dick period, what you talking about?"

Lord, he was pulling at my heartstrings. In my mind I'm thinking, "Don't do this. It's just sex. You don't even know this guy. You know nothing about him. He could be married. He could be a big liar." Then a small part of me wonders if he's telling the truth? What if he is exactly what I've been searching for forever? I don't even want to think about this anymore. I distract myself and prepare to give him the ride of his life.

We both laugh. He pulls out, and it's not as uncomfortable this time. He watches me, as we switch positions. His eyes seeming to stare into my soul. I return his look as I ease down slowly on his dick. We both inhale sharply and say fuck as I take more of his dick. I feel my pussy trying to accommodate his dick.

That's when I start moving. Slowly, up and down, swirling my hips in a circle, slowly. He grips my hips and I get on my tip toes. I get close to the top and I go down a little bit. With each downward motion, I attempt to take more and more of him. He's watching me, I'm watching him, and he pulls me closer to his chest.

"Spit in my mouth." he says.

So, I kiss him slowly and I make it juicy. He takes some of it and asks for more. He slaps my ass hard and that not only makes me kiss him deeper and more sloppily, I take more of his dick too. Fuck, his dick is so wide. Thick thick. My pussy is throbbing and aching. Im gonna take all of this dick or die trying. Let's hope I don't regret that tomorrow. I feel some wobbly legs in my future. By the time I'm able to put all of him inside me, I've caught a rhythm, and he's matching me thrust for thrust. The room is filled with sounds of "shit", "fuck", "that's it", and "don't stop". His stomach is getting all wet up. I'm gliding on his dick. It's almost like my pussy wants to reject his dick, the way she's squeezing and pushing against him.

"Damn this pussy so good. Keep fucking me. That's it. You think you can take all this dick? Come on baby you can do it."

He's squeezing my ass tightly and slapping both cheeks without warning. Each slap seems to make me even wetter. I feel my cum building and I close my eyes, and I let the feeling wash over me. One of his hands move off my ass while the other spreads one cheek open. He puts one finger at my asshole, and starts moving it in a circular motion. In my mind I'm begging him to do it please. I love it. He seems to read my mind and inserts one finger in my ass. I throw my head back.

"Don't stop."

I pick up speed on his dick, as his finger matches my pace.

"Don't stop, don't stop, I'm about to cum. Please, please."

My body stiffens up, my pussy latches on to his dick, and just when my asshole tightens, he puts two fingers in my ass. I scream out, and I cum and I cum and I shake and quiver. Fuck. I lay against his chest, and my body is still trying to stop the aftershocks. He kisses me softly.

"Baby we not through yet, he says, Daddy still needs to cum."

Oh my god, this is not anything I'm used to at all.

I murmur some unintelligible word and he flips me on my back. He's inside me with one quick thrust. My pussy is swelling up. Literally. I can feel it.

"Damn baby. You so tight."

I'm so not used to getting fucked like this. At all. This will last me a year at least unless we continue this in the future. He is wearing my ass out. He increases his speed, and I swear I'm trying to match his motions. My body is in autopilot while I have one eye closed. His dick gets harder and harder as he puts the whole thing inside of me. My hands dig into his back as I moan loudly into his ear.

"Kevin please. Let me swallow your cum. I need it. I love the way it tastes. Please baby."

That's definitely my go to, when I can't take anymore dick. He stiffens up, pulls out quickly and I beg him for it.

"Get over here beautiful, and get all your cum."

I hurriedly get on my knees and swallow every ounce while looking up at him. He looks down at me, with his mouth open and sweat dripping from his forehead.

"Damn girl. Where the fuck did you come from?"

Chapter 3

BOFFUM

The way we all met was funny. Ironic even. I'm trying to protect the innocent and none of us ever even asked the other if we were involved or potentially belonged to someone else. I don't even know if it would have mattered at the time. Still, I don't need my windows busted out, my tires flattened, or anybody coming to me as a woman so both of these guys will have an alias. I also won't be describing them exactly as they truly look in real life. Comprende? So, the dark skin guy is Midnight, which is fitting of course, and the lighter brown skin guy is Chris. I picked Chris for him because he reminded me of a more rugged Chris Brown. Like how Chris would look if he grew up in the hood, never became famous, and rarely looked inviting even when he smiled. Quite honestly, he kind of reminded me of Dave East when he isn't smiling. Definitely more menacing looking than Chris Brown, but in a good way. Midnight was about 5'10", and Chris was 6'2". Midnight was solid, meaning he had nice big arms, nice shoulders and thighs, with a nice midsection. He worked out, but you could tell he had slacked off for a lil bit. So, his stomach wasn't flat, but it didn't have rolls or anything. He probably weighed about 225. I preferred dudes with weight on them. He had tattoo sleeves on both arms and the night I met him, he had a bottom gold plate in. His tattoo guy was phenomenal, because even as dark as he was, they still showed up well against his skin. That's what caught my eye in the first place. His tattoos and his grill. I was a sucker for grills and dark skin men. He smelled so good too. A clean scent that lingered after he walked away. Pretty white teeth with a dazzling smile. He had this sexy ass vibe and walk about him, a very confident stride. He's the type of guy I'd always admire from afar while simultaneously hoping he'd say something to me. Lord knows I never approached men. Not back then anyway. Letting my thoughts wander at what it would be like between his thighs, or sitting on top of them, or under those arms. Chris would be considered red, or light skin. I wasn't usually attracted to men of a lighter complexion, but he had this sexy inviting energy. He was slimmer than I liked them, lanky even, but he definitely had nice arms. He looked like he went to the gym regularly. His arms fit his physique. His beard was perfect. There was no other way to describe it. He was tatted up all over, neck and both legs included. He had a pretty smile that was a little crooked in the front, but it added to his charm. He had nice long fingers with clean short fingernails. I liked that. I always have. A man's hands always mattered to me. He smelled good too, but it wasn't a scent that was familiar to me. I usually knew men's cologne, but I couldn't place his. Later I'd find out that he had his own signature scent. An oil that he made specifically tailored with the scents he loved. So, it all started on a sleepless night, as I tossed and turned in bed, which turned into me deciding to go to a 24-hour laundromat. I lived in a nice apartment complex, but the machines were all out of order for the weekend. I had already waited last minute to wash my clothes, and I had nothing else clean, except of course the endless brand-new clothes in my closet that I never found places to wear. I was hoping one day I would. In fact, I was here in the laundromat in my yoga pants, Tupac shirt, furry slides, no panties, and an All Money In cap, and my Chanel glasses. I had a loose wave layered sew in going on that I had up in a ponytail. I wasn't expecting to meet anyone, let alone fuck them. It had to be 1:30 in the morning. I thought the place would be deserted, and I'd have it all to myself. I actually did for the first 15 minutes. Most people on Friday or Saturday nights were out trying to have a good time. Sunday was usually the day most people remembered they had to wash clothes. Midnight walked in with 2 baskets stacked on top of one another. He went back out to get his detergent, bleach and fabric softener. I really liked the way he walked. Very confident and sexy. Masculine energy on 10 but not in a conceited way. It was alluring. Like he knew his power. I definitely loved that. I was waiting on my loads in the washer as he was loading his in. We glanced at each other and he nodded his head at me, and I did a little wave. The whole head nod thing wasn't me. I felt slightly uncomfortable under his gaze, so I quickly looked away. I knew he was checking me out, and I was blushing hard from that hoping my glasses were hiding it. My earbuds were in and I was jamming to Blue Laces 2 by Nipsey Hussle. It's one of my favorite songs by him. I was also flipping an Essence magazine with Jada Pinkett-Smith, her daughter Willow and her mom on the cover. Per usual, I was in my own little world, oblivious to anyone else. Actually, not entirely. I was aware of Midnight's energy, I was just trying to ignore him. My body was reacting to a complete stranger, and I didn't understand it and didn't wanna dissect it right now. I was so engrossed in reading the article after tuning him out that I didn't hear anything, and I had momentarily forgot about my loads of clothes. I felt his energy before he got close. The energy that I was trying to avoid. I looked up at him when he was almost close enough to reach out and touch me. His lips were moving, and that in itself was a distraction. Pretty brown at the top and a dusky pink at the bottom. He had a nice goatee as well. He pointed to his ears and I removed my earbuds.

"Sorry, I didn't mean to disturb you, but your machine stopped a few minutes ago. I figured you didn't want to be in here all night, so I thought I'd let you know."

"Thanks."

I was openly staring at this man. He was gorgeous.

"Sorry, I'm Nicki.."

And as I said before y'all, let's call him Midnight. He extended his hand, and I shook it.

"Nice to meet you."

Now he was staring at me. The temperature went up about 10 degrees. Lord. There was that energy again. What exactly was this energy? I wasn't used to immediate attraction to anyone. He finally let my hand go, ("No don't let go yet," I sighed inside) then he smiled at me.

"My bad, I'll let you get back to it."

Part of me wanted him to touch more than my hands. I wanted to look down in those hazel eyes, at least they looked hazel in this light as he ate my pussy. That thought had me blushing and I could feel my ears and my face getting hotter. He still was staring at me. I was so ashamed. I prayed he couldn't read minds or sense my reaction to him. That sounds animalistic in a way. As if he could sense my arousal and catch my scent. But anyway, I went back to my clothes and started taking them out of the washer. I bent to put them back in the baskets I had when he brought over one of the facility baskets.

"Thank you. This will be easier."

He didn't move, he just kept staring at me. It was really starting to make me uncomfortable. Not in a bad way though. In a "I'm wondering if my pants will be wet since I don't have on any panties" kind of way.

"Where is your man? Why are you here alone in the middle of the night? It could be dangerous for you. The world is a scary place nowadays."

"Well I guess you're right, you never truly know what could happen. But I am semi prepared."

I hold up my key chain that also has pepper spray on it. He smiles and nods. He held the dryer doors open for me as I added the clothes. His hand lightly grazed mine as our hand touched the handle at the same time. In that moment, I got chills all over my body. I looked in his hazel eyes, they really were hazel, and he was staring back into my brown ones. His lips parted slightly, and my mouth went dry. Lord, this fine ass man was turning me on. And I knew I had the same effect on him. At least I hoped. I didn't want to look down and catch a glimpse of any print. That seemed crass. Plus, I didn't want to be tempted to drop to my knees and suck his dick. Lord. I was in here acting like I was in heat. My face was so hot. I was so horny I thought that I had to be ovulating. But nothing could come of this. I didn't know him. I couldn't just give in to my basic carnal instincts. Or could I? The spark between us was heightening. We were standing close to each other when his washers stopped. His scent made me want to get really close to him. He turned his back to me to remove the clothes from the washers, and at that precise moment, the door chimed and in walked another guy. I watched him as he walked in. His height garnered my attention at first but the closer he came to me, the more I felt his energy too and something deep down in my gut began to thump and purr. Midnight had finished loading his clothes in the dryer and when he turned around, he glanced at this guy and they both dapped it up. I had to ask.

"Do you two know each other?"

They both laughed.

"We're roommates."

"Oh."

In my mind I was thinking that was the end of that. Two fine ass men in the middle of the night that actually know each other. What are the odds? I put my earbuds in and turned back to my magazine. No sense in fantasizing. Nothing was going to happen, so I retreated back to my private bubble. I was definitely disappointed. Especially because Midnight was giving me nasty thoughts. I wished that when we were touching, even though it was brief, I was imagining that he actually kissed me in that moment. And now that this other dude was here, it seemed he'd thrown cold water on my little fantasy. I became engrossed in my magazine and music. I tuned both of their asses out. After about 15 minutes, I realized that they both were looking at me and actually having a conversation about me as they both watched me. Midnight did the ear motion again so this time, I just turned my music all the way down and left it that way. Both were looking bashful, so I knew that something was going on. What could they both say at the same time to me? No way they both wanted me or even considered me attractive. I was about to be proved wrong.

"We see you here by yourself, and your clothes are almost done. We are both off tomorrow, so if you want, why don't you come through in an hour? Our clothes will be done by then, and we only live like 15 minutes away. It'll just be us two, if you wanted to come through and chill with us. Our place has a nice little vibe. We're in a nice little gated community, with plenty security. I don't know what you're into, but we got something to smoke on, and we keep something to sip on."

"Y'all want me to come through on some chill shit huh? But I don't know y'all. Y'all could be crazy, or serial killers or rapists."

"I promise you, we are none of the above. We can both show you our ids, you can get our tag numbers, and you have control of everything. You can keep whatever you want on you, your phone too of course, and leave whenever you want. Matter of fact one of our neighbors is a detective. Look him up too. Officer Brian Childress. Look on our social media pages. Oh, I'm Chris. I know Midnight introduced himself already. We're good guys, we were just thinking you should come hang out with us. None of us are doing anything this weekend. It's the middle of the night, so why not just hang?"

I just looked them both in the eye. They wrote down everything. Address, tag numbers, phone numbers, and gate code. I was off on the weekends anyway and didn't have to be back to work until Monday. I shrugged my shoulders and said what the hell. I told them to give me an hour and a half. I went home and took a quick shower, ditched my glasses and put my contacts in. I brushed my teeth, but I didn't get all dressy. I threw on a Ripped Marilyn Monroe shirt, and some baggy fitting army fatigue cargos, that went a little over my knees. I redid my ponytail and put on some lip gloss. I wasn't gonna get too dolled up just to go chill with two men who already knew what I looked like on a bad day. Only an hour had passed by the time I made it to the gate. I put the code in and drove in like I knew where I was going. Looking at this place, I understood why they were roommates. This area was quite affluent. Definitely upscale. These townhomes weren't cheap. Security wasn't asleep even this late at night. I was riding around following GPS to 1206 Sunset Lanes Circle. It was well lit, even in the middle of the night. All I saw were Audi's, BMWs, Volkswagens, and Mercedes. This was definitely a step up from where I lived. Chris opened the door after I knocked three times.

"Come on in. We were wondering if you were going to show."

The look he gave me definitely thawed my nerves. He led me to a bar they had off to the left side. I was looking around as I followed him because wow. How much was the rent here? Or did they own this townhouse? So many questions but I didn't want to be intrusive. High ceilings, hardwood floors, and marble countertops. Burgundy sandal wood, and dark blue were the color scheme. No carpet, just plush throw rugs everywhere. Nice décor that had me feeling like someone else decorated this place. It definitely was a vibe. It smelled very clean in here. Not like a bleach, Pine-Sol and Fabuloso scent, but more of a clean scented candle or house warmer scent. I didn't see any candles burning yet though. Perhaps they had the plug ins or the warmers. Chris was walking around slowly, making sure I was taking it all in.

"You smoke?"

"Nah."

"I have edibles too if you prefer those."

"Nah i'm good."

"Would you like a drink?"

"I'll take some patron on ice if you have it."

"I gotcha. You want salt and lime?"

"Sure. You make me feel like I'm at a real bar."

"Actually, I moonlight sometimes as a bartender. "

"Nice, I wouldn't have thought that."

"Why not? I work hard."

He laughed and winked at me.

"Mmmhmmm. Of course, you do."

We both laughed easily.

"After I make you this drink, I'll show you where we were before you knocked. Midnight is down there setting the room up now. He's definitely lit already. We were both smoking since we got here. We about to watch I got the Hook Up 2, unless you wanted to just listen to music and vibe."

"I have been meaning to watch that movie. I'll watch it with y'all."

He made my drink perfectly. It was definitely a heavily poured double shot at least. I was licking the salt on the rim as we walked to the end of this softly lit hallway and reached a door off to the left. It was definitely darker in here with soft lights in the corners. No cords were hanging anywhere to be seen. It was definitely set up well. The tv had to be at least 72 inches. The black leather sectional was nice and there were recliners on both ends. Each recliner had its own cupholder and remote. It was really cozy. Midnight was working the remote. His eyes were definitely red and he looked even better than he had at the laundromat, definitely more relaxed. That made my nerves disappear. Both of their energy had me at ease, as crazy as that sounds. This time Midnight had on a wife beater and some gray sweatpants. I definitely was sneaking some peeks. He was at least 6 inches while flaccid. I sipped on my drink slowly. I was trying to devoid my thoughts of filth. Let's see how long that lasted. Chris came in a few minutes later and sat on the end of the sectional , on the right side of me. Midnight sat right beside me, on my left. Midnight started the movie, looked over at me and smiled. Lord help me. I emptied my glass faster than I thought I would. Chris offered to make me another one. I agreed. I wasn't even tipsy yet. He came back in record time. He really was good at this. He made me want to tip him. Both of theirs scents were unique. I still was leaning toward Midnight. I was so attracted to him. However I did steal some glances at Chris. He was very handsome. He just wasn't my usual type. But something about him was intriguing. I'm not sure at what point that Midnight put his hand on my thigh. It had been there for at least a few minutes before I noticed it was there. I looked at his hands before looking in his eyes. He winked at me. My God he was so sexy. I wanted to suck on his lips and lick his neck and nipples. I try to focus back on the movie. Probably about 45 minutes in, I start feeling good and relaxed. I have a slight buzz going on. I caught Midnight's eyes, staring at me and biting his lips slightly. My God he was so fucking sexy. I wonder if his cum was sweet? I sigh and focus back on the movie. Not completely tipsy yet but just about there. Chris excuses himself, and I don't even care where he's headed. Midnight's hand was still on my left thigh, but it had shifted much higher up. I was feeling so good that it didn't even bother me. Here I was In the home of two fine ass man, getting turned on. Yolo right? Midnight took his tank off, and Chris returned from wherever he had escaped to. He handed me another drink even though I didn't ask for one. I look up at him and raise my eyebrows.

"I figured you'd want another one, the way you gulped that last one down."

"I did actually, but this will be my last one."

"Ok cool. Let me know if you change your mind."

He took his seat at the opposite end, but also took his shirt off. Somehow, collectively the energy shifted in the room. It was almost like we'd all agreed that we were going to have sex. Midnight picked up the remote and changed the channel. Most would try to incorrectly label this as a train. Nothing could be further from the truth. This was about to be an intimate threesome, and these men were about to please me like I was their queen. I pulled my shirt over my head. Midnight said, come on now, don't be shy. I unhooked my bra and stripped down to my lace boy shorts. Everything next seemed to happen in slow motion. Midnight grabbed me and started kissing me slowly. His tongue tasted so good. Weed, mixed with alcohol, mixed with some sweet mint, with his natural flavor intertwined. It was heavenly. I started sucking on his tongue. As I was kissing him, Chris was watching us occasionally, while sipping his drink and smoking but giving the movie more attention. I'm so aware of Chris watching us and it's really turning me on. After a few minutes, I realize that they've stopped the movie and put on porn. All I was hearing was moaning. Midnight began moving my hair tie from the ponytail it was in. I felt my hair brushing up against the middle of my back. His hands began stroking my back then I felt soft kisses against my neck. His kisses turned into licks. Slow wet licks, that made me hunger for more. Having his hands against my skin was unlike anything I had ever felt before. His hands had calluses like a man that worked hard, but his touch was gentle. Midnight began palming my breasts, stroking my nipples. I felt his lips surround my nipple and I sighed and watched him as he licked, sucked and nibbled. It didn't even bother me that Chris was watching us. In all actuality, it was making this even better. I enjoy watching and being watched. I offered Midnight my other breast. He took his time with each one. He's sucking on one breast while my eyes are closed. I smell Chris' scent, and feel his energy before he touched me. He takes my other breast and starts licking and sucking my nipple. They both are at my breasts like they're hoping for milk. Both hands on my body, both tongues, and me absorbing all of this. I'm moaning and stroking both of their heads.

"Them panties need to come off, now."

Chris pauses after he says that. Midnight pauses too and helps me out of my panties.

"Damn, I need that fat pussy in my mouth," Chris says.

I sit back on the sofa, with my legs open wide. Chris gets on his knees and starts slowly rubbing my pussy.

"Damn bruh, her pussy pretty as fuck."

They both are putting my pussy on display, and I've never felt more seen, wanted, and desired. Chris slips a finger inside me, and Midnight starts kissing me. As he's kissing me, his hands are stroking my breasts and my back. Chris puts his tongue on my clit and licks it so softly. My moans are louder than the flick that's playing.

Midnight kisses me softly twice more before pulling away. Chris makes a groan that says he doesn't wanna stop tasting me. I definitely don't want him to, but we need more room. After a few more licks, he reluctantly stops. Midnight looks at us both and says, *"Let's go to my bed."*

He looked me in my eyes, and my look said it all. We all stand up and follow Midnight down the hall and to the left. The entire walk Chris is gripping my ass, and whispering in my ear that he can't wait to taste my cum. We make it to Midnight's room, and he looks at us both and I go to him. I kiss him and Chris is behind me, spreading my legs, and I feel his lips on my pussy and ass. He starts tongue fucking my ass and it feels so damn good. Midnight kisses me slowly, wraps his hands around my neck and squeezes. I love that shit. He drops one hand and starts fingering me. I'm overcome with sensation. I've never done anything like this, and I see more of this in my future. Quick glances around the room and I notice his bed is a California king bed with leopard designed sheets. Chris is behind me going into overdrive on my ass, and that's when Midnight adds another finger inside me, as he chokes me.

"Fuck, I yell out. Don't either one of you fucking stop."

Chris mumbles something, and Midnight smirks at me.

"You're gonna cum for us?"

"Fuck yes, just don't stop."

Midnight lets go of my neck and keeps his fingers inside me. But then he gets on his knees in front of *me. I look down at him in surprise. I whimper his name.*

"We're gonna give you everything you need tonight."

He continues to finger me, and then he starts sucking my clit, as Chris is eating my ass. This is so intense. I'm yelling out fuck every few seconds. I'm not going to last much longer. The thickness of Midnight's rough fingers and the wetness of his mouth on my clit, combined with the wetness of Chris tongue in my ass has me wanting to convulse. All you hear is wetness, smacking noises and two men moaning as they taste me. When I start to cum, Chris goes even deeper in my ass and I put my hand on his head as I keep him right there. My release coats Midnights fingers, and yet he continues softly licking my clit. When the spasms stop, I feel Chris behind me, standing now, and he lets me lean up against him. He kisses my neck and asks if I want more? More? Shit yes. Midnight takes me by the hand, and we all get in the bed. He moves to the middle of the bed, and I look down at his pretty big thick dick. I wanna return the favor. I crawl to him, staying on my knees. I take him in my mouth slowly, and he exhales sharply when I start sucking him faster. While I'm sucking his dick and licking everywhere, he'll allow, Chris is behind me, stroking my pussy and ass. I hear him ripping open a condom and a few seconds later, he's pushing deep inside me. He leaves a finger in my ass. I'm moaning and groaning and trying to keep Midnight in my mouth. We all have a rhythm after a few minutes. I've arched my back and Midnight is letting me have my way with him.

Midnight talks to me like Wesley Pipes when I suck his dick and I love every word.

"You love sucking dick, don't you? With yo pretty ass. Use some more spit on that dick. Wet my shit up. There you go. Suck that dick. I've been wanting to put it in yo life since I first saw you. Yessss. Deep throat that shit. You a nasty girl huh? I like that shit. You keep sucking my dick like that and I'm gonna fill your pretty mouth up with cum. That's what you

want isn't it? You like to swallow nut? You look like you do."

He slowly strokes my face.

"Answer me sexy. You want my cum?"

"Yes, all of it."

At least I try to say that with a mouthful of his dick.

"I'm gonna give you what you want."

He starts holding my head, lifting his hips up, and starts throwing his dick deeper in my mouth and down my throat. Chris starts fucking me faster and his finger inside my ass speeds up too. It's like we're all in sync. I feel another orgasm coming and we all seem to be even breathing the same. Chris puts his finger in my ass as deep as it'll go and is slamming his dick deep inside my pussy. He's so hard and long. Much longer than I've ever had, and he's digging deep. I taste Midnights cum in my mouth, just as I began to cum. The clenching of my pussy against Chris dick is all he needs to go over the edge. He yells out "*fucccck*". Then we're all in unison like a chorus. It feels so damn good, I don't want this to stop. Midnight fills my mouth up with cum, and Chris fills the condom up, as my pussy leaks. Chris pulls out of me, and I miss him already when he does. I get beside Midnight, and he reaches over, and grabs something already rolled by the bed.

"Mind if I smoke?"

"It's cool."

Chris looks at us, and smiles.

"I'll leave y'all to it."

"You leaving?"

"Yeah, I'll see you in the morning though."

He winks as he leaves, and a part of me doesn't want him to go. He walks out and shuts the door with a soft click, and Midnight and I are alone. He extends his hand, and asks if I want to smoke. I look down and notice that his pretty dick is getting hard again. I shake my head, and stare into his beautiful eyes,

"I want more."

"So do I he says. Come here, sit on this dick."

I do just that. I'm on my knees, and I ease down slowly on his dick, and he moans out, and cuffs my ass.

"Damn."

"Yesssss. Fuck."

I put my hands around his neck and begin to lightly choke him as I ride his dick. The look he gives me is one of trust and certainty, a look that says he hasn't done this before, but he's with it. I increase the pressure on both sides of his neck. I'm speeding up with each stroke and making sure I go all the way down his dick, squeezing my pussy muscles. His heads falls back and he squeezes my waist tightly.

"Fuck. Don't stop. Ride that motherfucking dick, with your sexy ass."

I'm squeezing my pussy muscles and ass muscles too, making each cheek jump as I stroke his dick with my pussy. His mouth is slightly open, and those gold grills are shining. They sexy af. I leave one hand on his neck, and the other I put against his chest for leverage.

"Damn your dick is so deep inside me. Fuck. I needed this."

He looks in my eyes, leans forward, and starts licking and kissing on my nipples. I leave the one hand on his neck, and with my other hand, I reach back and start fingering my own ass. I let go of his neck and take that hand and hold my ass open. He's looking at me in amazement.

"You so fucking nasty, and I love that shit. Keep fingering that tight ass."

I do exactly as he says. I'm moaning, he's moaning, and we're both starting to sweat. He puts his arms around me lifting me up and slamming me on the dick. This feels so good, I forget all about fingering my ass. I lean close towards him and put my arms around his back and hold on tight. He was definitely strong as fuck. He looks up at me and I look down at him. We kiss softly, then it speeds up. I don't think I'll be able to walk straight tomorrow. I am just about drained.

"I'm gonna cum, where do you want it baby?"

"I wanna swallow it. All of it, please."

He smirks at me, and motions for me to hop off. I hop off and I'm on my knees in front of him waiting.

"Open that pretty fucking mouth wide."

I open my mouth, and his cum shoots down my throat. He gives me a throat full and I swallow it all down, sticking my tongue out afterwards to show that all his cum is gone. He lays back on the bed and I scoot beside him and lay my head on his chest. He leans down and kisses my forehead. We snuggle like this for what seems like a few seconds. It's actually about a couple hours or so. We wake up to the sun beginning to rise. I look up at him and he's looking at me and he raises his eyebrow.

"Round two?"

"I was thinking the same thing."

Chapter 4

DADDY

I spent almost all day lying in bed on social media. Waiting on him to come home. Another late night I suppose. I didn't much get on Facebook anymore and I had been nosey on Instagram all day. Laughing my ass off at the comments on The Shade Room. I decided to jump on my favorite app, Twitter. It seemed everyone on my timeline was in a horny mood this evening. Porn up and down my timeline, people wanting dick to be dropped off, and waiting for someone to come ride their face. I was pretty entertained. I lost track of time. I started joining in on this thread about dominance and submission. It seemed a lot of men were becoming more submissive these days. I got on the thread saying I wanted to be dominated and completely controlled. Whipped, handcuffs, tied up, gagged, and I wanted a belt used. A few men offered to come through and do just that. But as usual, they were states away and besides, I had someone. It seemed like it was in title only these days. We hadn't fucked in a while. A few quickies here and there but no intense fucking. Not the pressure that I needed that would stop this ache. Quick kisses in the morning, nothing slow, sloppy or wet. Nothing lingering. Even the quickies seemed to get me turned on, then he would be finished as soon as I was getting into it. It wasn't enough. Not anymore. I needed more. I will admit, my responses to these men went beyond harmless flirting. But I'd never go all the way. I was just a big tease. It turned me on knowing that I could turn random men on. They'd never see me in real life. It was just talk. The equivalent of the talk men do when they're locked up. The kind of talk that I needed from the one I was with. Where was he anyway? All these late nights. Hell, he may be cheating. Who knows? Maybe I should go beyond flirting. (Sighs) But I loved his big-headed self.

    I started to get really turned on with this back and forth sexual banter between me and one of my followers. I went and ran a bath and put on my fuck me playlist. Immersing myself in the water felt so good. I had my faux locs pinned up. I had already been waxed and exfoliated to perfection yesterday. My dark chocolate skin was silky smooth. I put my back against the headrest in our oversized jacuzzi tub and relaxed. The more Would You Mind by Janet Jackson played, the more turned on I got. Before I knew it, my right hand was on my pussy. My left hand was spreading my pussy lips open. I started to moan as soon as I rubbed my clit. This is where I wanted his mouth and his tongue. I wanted his pressure on me. The weight of his body when he was on top of me, looking in my eyes, brown eyes staring back at brown, seeing my soul. His cappuccino colored skin against my chocolate. He's a little over 6'3" and reminded me of Michael Ealy, with a more rugged look. Just picture Michael Ealy in For Colored Girls the movie. Like that with brown eyes, about 25 more pounds, and dreads that went to his shoulder. My handsome man. All mine. Damn I loved him. I needed him. My fingers and my vibrators weren't enough anymore. It seemed that I was using them at least four or five times a week. I needed him. I looked down at my fingers like I was tired of using them. If they could speak, they'd probably say, *"Girl, when are you gonna give me a break, damn?"* I stopped caressing myself. Fuck this. He was going to give me some dick tonight damn it. I was tired of getting myself off all the time. I could have stayed single for this shit. I had a whole man and had to make myself cum. This was some ghetto shit. I rolled my eyes. So pathetic. Damn him.

I soaked for a few more minutes, scrubbed up, then rinsed off with the handheld shower. I rubbed his favorite smelling lotion of mine, Light Blue, by Dolce and Gabbana, and stepped into a black lace teddy. I didn't have much for breasts. I was almost a C cup, with the padding of course. Yet thanks to genetics, I was quite curvy, or thick most would say. Which these days meant small waist, wide hips and fat ass. Exactly how he liked it. I slipped my feet into my furry house slippers. I looked down at my fresh pedicure. He loved when I got white on my toes. I liked soft neutral colors too, but I liked pleasing him sometimes. I checked the time, 9:55. I put my black silk robe on and went downstairs for a big glass of wine. I headed back upstairs, got back in bed and back on Twitter. The guy I was having a conversation with was slightly handsome. He had pretty hands, clean nails and a big dick. Don't ask me how I knew. Let's just say, my DMs were never dry. From dick pictures to cum videos. All from random men who didn't even know my name. I kinda loved the anonymity.

"Show me what that pussy looks like."

"I told you, I'm with someone. We live together. I can't send you pictures or videos of my pussy. You know this."

"Well, where is he? You always home alone? It doesn't seem like he appreciates what he has. If you give me a chance, I'll treat you much better than him."

I don't know how he figured that, considering that he was states away. It sounded good though. I sipped my wine and responded that he was at work. I was always multitasking and was on Twitter and Instagram at the same time. I was watching a clip of a gym workout that a celebrity had posted. I got a notification that I had a message in my DM, a video actually. It was from the same guy. I opened it, and just stared at it. It was him. Jacking his dick. Again. I pressed play, and he's moaning, and jacking his dick slowly.

"You like this big dick, don't you? Mmmhmm. You know you wanna feel this big black ass dick. I already know that pussy is wet. Probably tight as fuck too. Come get you some of this dick. Sexy ass."

He kept jacking it slowly and making eye contact with the camera. My clit was jumping uncontrollably. I couldn't pull my eyes away. Don't stop I'm saying like he could hear me. Fuck. Cum for me baby. It was like he heard me. His pace increased faster and faster, and he came. So much, so thick, everywhere. Fuck.

"Lick it up. Every last drop. You know you want to. Open your fucking mouth for this cum."

My mouth went dry. I almost choked drinking that wine so fast. Fuck. I needed some dick. As I was about to reply to his video, my iPhone started ringing. Finally! He better not tell me no bullshit ass story. I just needed to know when his ass was coming home. He could stay at work if he wanted to. Just so long as he dropped that dick off.

"Hi."

"Don't fucking say hi to me. You must have forgot that I follow you on all your fucking social media pages. If you wanted to be sneaky, you should have made a fake page. Why you trying me with this bullshit?"

"Babe, what are you talking about?"

"Oh, so you're gonna act innocent. Who the fuck is @biggerthed4u33? You talking to that nigga in the DM? You planning to meet up with him? Answer me. I'm not playing with you."

"Babe, calm down. It's not like that, I promise."

"Have you answered his dm or not? You think I'm stupid? Yes or no?"

"Only a few, but baby—"

"You fucking that nigga?"

"What? No. It was just harmless flirting babe, I promise. I have never met him. I never talked to him in real life. He has never even heard my voice, I promise."

"But you wanted to fuck him? Tell me the fucking truth."

"Babe no, I promise. "

"He turned you on, my pussy got wet for another nigga?"

"What? Babe."

"Oh, you deaf now? Did my pussy get wet for this nigga?"

"Babe please."

"Nah, it ain't no babe please. You been chatting it up with this nigga in the DM. You flirting with this nigga like you don't have a fucking man. Fuck you talking bout! You was gonna fuck this nigga. Don't bullshit me."

"Babe, I swear I wasn't. I only want you. I promise. Babe please listen to me —"

"Nah fuck that. I'm on my fucking way. I want you upstairs in the bedroom, naked, and on your fucking knees."

"Baby please."

"Did you hear what the fuck I said?"

"Yes."

"Yes, what?"

"Yes Daddy."

"Exactly. Be on your fucking knees."

He hung up in my face. My pussy was throbbing. I knew that he knew his effect on me. We hadn't played in a long time. I went upstairs with my wine glass in hand, refilled of course, and was about to take off my lingerie, then I thought he'd think it was sexier if I kept it on. I gulped the last of the Riesling. I went in the bathroom, brushed my teeth and rinsed with some mouthwash. I looked at my reflection in the mirror. Damn I looked sexy. I heard his truck pulling up in the garage. Damn that was fast. He had to have already been on the way home when he called. I took off my robe and got on my knees. I heard him close the door and let the garage door down. I couldn't hear anything for a few minutes, but I was listening hard. I heard him coming up the stairs. I felt him before he came in. I felt his energy and his eyes on me.

"So you being real disobedient tonight I see. You like to get me riled up? This the game you wanna play? You wanna be punished?"

"I thought you'd like to see me in this."

"You thought I'd like to see you like in this what?"

"I thought you'd like to see me in this, Daddy.

"I do. But not tonight. That's not what the fuck I told you. Hardheaded ass. Stand up and take it off. Don't look at me either."

I turned my back to him once I stood up. I started taking it off, pulling it down my shoulders.

"Slow down. Let me watch you."

Fuck. I took it off slowly, touching my breasts, my pussy, and making my ass jiggle, even though I didn't need to do all that. I knew he loved that. I wanted him to keep his eyes on me.

"Get back on your fucking knees."

I got on my knees with my back to him. He didn't come to me, I heard him walk away and going into our walk-in closet. I heard boxes being moved around. What was he getting? I felt him by my side seconds later.

"You like disobeying me? Don't you?"

Before I could answer or react, he slapped my ass, with what felt like one of our whips.

"Answer me!"

Slap.

"Daddy please."

Slap.

"Answer me now."

Slap.

"No baby, I don't."

"No what?"

Slap

"No Sir, ummm. No Daddy."

"That's better. Why the fuck are you flirting with other men on social media? You wanted to piss me off?"

Slap

"No! Oww. No Daddy."

"Then why?"

Slap.

"Tell me."

Slap

"I—"

Slap.

"You what? Say it!"

Slap.

"Daddy please."

Slap.

"Ok! I just wanted your attention."

Slap.

"My attention? So, you answer DMs and flirt with other niggas? That was your way of getting my fucking attention?! You wanna fuck this nigga? He sent you pictures of his dick?"

"No! I promise, no. I wasn't gonna fuck him. Never."

Slap. Slap. Slap. Slap.

"Oh fuck. Owww. Daddy please, please. I'm sorry. I won't do this again."

Slap. Slap. Slap. Slap.

"You got damn right you won't."

I hear him throw the whip down and I'm grateful. My ass is on fire. He starts rubbing each cheek. Then he spreads them and puts his fingers between them slowly. Like he's searching for something he lost. He finds my pussy and I open my legs.

"Look at this. Pussy soaking fucking wet. For me or for that nigga?"

"Daddy please."

"Nah, it ain't no daddy please. This pussy better only get wet for Daddy."

He rubs my pussy lips, parts them, and puts two fingers inside of me. I gasp out loud, because his fingers are so long and thick, and they feel so good. He fingers me slow, and deep. I'm grinding my ass against his arm. As soon as I really start enjoying it, he pulls them away.

"Daddy no, please."

"Fuck that. You want pleasure? You want me to make you cum? You talking to, and flirting with other niggas, and you disobedient as fuck. I'm not gonna let you cum yet. You don't deserve to cum."

He sits on the bed and unbuckles his pants.

"Get over here."

I crawl over to him and watch him take out my dick. My beautiful black dick, with the perfect curve, and heavy balls. He looks at me in the eyes.

"You know what to do. Get to work."

I loved when he talked to me like this. I take him gently in my mouth. He grabs my hair and yanks my head back.

"Stop fucking playing with me. Suck this dick".

I get in the position that works best for me, when I'm attempting to swallow his dick, on my knees. I look him in his eyes, and I take so much of his dick down my throat, that my eyes are crying tears. I get a cute rhythm going, and I give it all I have. I test my limits and try to make all the dick disappear down my throat. I'm gagging on the dick and holding my breath, so I won't throw up, and I keep doing this over and over. Saliva is all on my breasts and thank God my hair is pinned up. I keep going. He strokes the side of my face lightly.

"Stop. I'm not gonna cum down your throat right now. You gotta wait to get this cum."

I suck a little more, and he gives me that dead serious look, so I stop.

"Come sit on this dick. Now."

I do as I'm told. Every time I get in this position it's like the first time. I have to adjust to the thickness of his dick. My pussy always feels like it's being stretched. Fuck. I love to take half of it. I never take all of it. I just can't.

"Tight ass pussy. Bounce that ass faster."

He's reached around in the bed and found the baby oil. He's pouring it on my ass, and rubbing some of it in. He's spreading my ass open, and the oil is everywhere. I get on my toes, and I'm squeezing the fuck out of his dick with my pussy. I needed this. I missed him fucking me like this.

I missed riding his dick. I don't want to stop. I feel his finger on my asshole. He knows I love this. Yes. God, yes.

"Please, please, Daddy please".

"Why should I? You think you deserve to cum? "

"Yes, Daddy please. I'm sorry. Please forgive me. I just wanted your attention. I just wanted you to punish me. I would never cheat on you, I'd never fuck anyone else. You know that."

I look him in his eyes. I want him to feel my sincerity.

"What do you want from Daddy?"

No matter how rough he is with me when we play like this, he's still gentle with me. He's still a man with a soft heart for me, and that's why I love him.

"Fuck me and put that anal vibrator in my ass. Please?"

"Beg. Beg me. Now."

With every movement on his dick, I beg. Over and over.

"Daddy please. I love you so much. Daddy please. Fuck me. Punish me. Please Daddy. Put it in my ass. Punish me. I love you. Please Daddy. "

"I'm gonna fuck the shit out of you. But you're gonna help me. You're gonna turn that vibrator on high and put it deep inside that tight lil asshole while I punish you with this dick. You won't stop until I tell you to. Do you hear me?"

"Yes Daddy, I promise. "

He lifts me a little and spreads my ass wide. He grips my thighs tightly, and we both lose our breath for a moment. He starts slamming me on his dick. I reach around and put the vibrator that's on high deep inside my asshole and it feels so good. The combination of him stretching my pussy, going deep inside me, and me fucking my ass is heaven. Just what

I needed.

"Daddy don't stop. Please. Don't stop. Make me cum so hard all over this dick, please Daddy. I love you so much. Fuck me Daddy. Fuck me hard, please please. "

He is giving me every inch of his dick. My pussy is feeling assaulted and stretched, and it's so fucking good. My asshole is so wet. My body is tingling. I'm shaking. I'm starting to sweat. I'm about to cum, and he knows it. He looks in my eyes, and we stare at each other for a few seconds.

"You're mine. Always. Do you hear me?"

"Yes Daddy. Yours. Always."

"Good. Cum for Daddy. "

He smacks my ass. That's all it takes. I cum so hard. Everywhere. It's like a dam bursting. I squirt all over him. It's dripping down his thighs and balls. I'm moaning and don't even realize the tears falling down my face. He takes the vibrator out of me.

"Come here."

He holds me close and kisses my forehead.

"I love you. But you're not done. Stay right here and don't move."

"Wait, what?"

He walks away from me and goes back into our closet. I hear movement, but not the boxes this time, he's pulling out the drawers from inside the chest. All of my vibrators, dildos, and toys are in there. My pussy starts throbbing at the anticipation of what he's about to do. I hear him walk out of the closet, and I hear his footsteps, then the light being turned on in the bathroom. What in the world is he doing? A few seconds later he's walking towards me, and I feel him as he gets closer. He grabs both of my arms and puts them behind my back. He starts wrapping my wrists together tightly, with what feels like rope. He ties it tightly. I feel a few seconds of fear. We've never went this far.

"Who do you submit to? "

"Daddy."

"Who else?"

"No one else. Only daddy."

"You will never embarrass me like this again. I'm about to make you remember who you submit to. You wanted my attention, you wanted me to fuck you, you open that pretty fucking mouth, and you beg daddy. You will never play games with me like this again. Ever. Tonight, I will claim you, and make you submit to me in a way you never have before."

That made me tremble inside. What was he talking about? I'm on the bed with my hands tied behind my back, and he bends me, so that my ass is in the air, and my face is in the covers. He adjusts a pillow under my head, to make my neck more comfortable.

"I ought to fucking gag you too but I'll be merciful tonight. "

My throat goes dry. Merciful? The ropes were starting to dig into my skin. I'd never felt so restrained. He starts rubbing my thighs and touching my pussy slowly. I hear him adjust in the bed. I feel his tongue on my clit and his chin up against my pussy. He's lying on his back and letting me ride his face. Being restrained while he does this is sexy as fuck but also unnerving. I really want to guide his fucking head. He laughs. He knows what I want. He stops and I hear him and feel him adjust again in the bed. He spreads my pussy lips like a flower. He's on his knees now, I can tell. He's sucking and spitting, moaning and caressing my pussy with his tongue. He's inhaling my scent and it's so erotic, I feel myself blushing. I feel so exposed, yet so desired, and wanted. I want to touch him, yank on his beard, but this restraint is so troublesome. It's driving me crazy.

"Baby untie me. Please."

He blatantly ignores me. He doesn't stop, just continues inhaling, tasting me and moaning.

"Daddy?"

"Mmm, fuck you taste so fucking good. Yes?"

"Please untie me, I crave to touch you."

"No. I'm just getting started. And you're being punished. Don't fucking forget that. You will submit to me."

"Daddy please, you know I submit to you. Always."

"Hush. Not like this. Never like this."

Now i'm worried a little. I trust him though. But what does he have up his sleeve? He stops tasting me and spreads my legs wider. Then he opens my ass cheeks up, then I feel his beard, his breath, then his tongue, there. I'm used to a finger there, a vibrator there, but not his tongue. I'm still, so still, taking it all in. This sensation is different than anything else. My ass is getting wet, and this feels so foreign yet I'm enjoying every second. Then I begin to moan and attempt to move. Closer to his mouth, his tongue. It's so different, and so wet and so good. My asshole has a throbbing pulse, like my clit and pussy does. How have I never felt that before? I'm in awe. I'm loving it. I want to act a fool all against his face. But these damn restraints are getting in the way of everything. Fuck. It's so good. He starts fingering my pussy, with what feels like 2 fingers. This. This is too much. I can't take this. No way. No fucking way. This will definitely make me submit. He continues and he speeds it up. We both have a rhythm now. Me attempting to give him full access, him driving me crazy, my bound wrists screaming in agony. Then I feel it. I know I'm gonna cum so fucking hard. He keeps going deeper with his hands, and I know I'm going to squirt. I pant. I yell. I shake, shudder, and scream. I feel his tongue inside my ass, and that's it. I unleash like a dam bursting. And I can't stop. I don't even understand how I have anything left to squirt. I'm so drained. It's everywhere. On him, his face, his beard. The sheets are a fucking mess. I fall over to the side panting and depleted.

"It's not over yet."

My eyes open wide. And then I know, I realize what he's going to do. I've secretly wanted to do this, wanted to try. I never thought he was into it. We never talked about it. He got up from the bed, and I hear him walking. A drawer opens, then closes. Seconds later, he's beside me. I hear him squeezing what I just know is lube, in his hands. He spreads my ass cheeks and coats my asshole. He removes his hand, yet I still hear friction, so I can only assume that he is coating himself. Lathering his dick up for my virgin ass. I'm preparing for what I know will be painful mentally. He starts rubbing a finger down my ass, which feels good. He slowly puts a finger in my ass, and quickly adds another. I love this. He knows I do. I'm moaning and rocking against his fingers.

"Please Daddy. Please let me touch you."

I feel him moving in bed, while his fingers work magic inside my ass.

"No. You will learn to submit to me. You will never behave the way you did today. You are mine. Say it."

"I'm yours. I promise. Daddy it's so good. I ache. Fuck me or suck on this pussy. I wanna cum again."

He slaps my ass, and I yell out in surprise.

"You're always so greedy and so needy."

"Please. I ache. I—"

Before I can say anything more, he removes his fingers and yanks my ass up in the air. Then I feel an intense stretching and pressure against my ass. It borders between pleasure and pain. I take deep breaths.

"That's it. Relax that asshole for Daddy."

He keeps pushing slowly, slowly. It's hurting now. But a part of me wants to see how bad it'll get. I like pain. He pushes more as I'm being stretched and opened for him. Then something happens. He's halfway in and it's starting to feel good. He pushes in further and it's too much.

"Wait. Stop. Don't move Daddy, let me adjust to you."

He stops. I breathe and breathe a few more times. I relax and exhale against the covers. I stay in this exposed position, with my wrists tied, and I wait. He moves slowly, this time he's taking it out and putting it back in. Each time, a little more dick. I'm adjusting to this assault on my ass. It's such a tight fit, the sensations are so much. I moan, I attempt to thrash, but as i'm getting used to it I feel like this is what I needed all along.

"That tight ass getting wet. Fuck me back. Throw it on Daddy."

I attempt to do just that. But I'm moving slowly. I feel his dick getting harder and he's moaning and starting to pull my hair. He picks up the pace. His thighs are smacking against my ass. He spreads my legs even wider, if that's possible, and presses my back down. My face is buried in the covers as I turn my head to the side so I can breathe. This stretching, the pleasure and pain, is so intense. The sensation is different than vaginally. It's indescribable almost. But I want more. I need more. I give him better access to my ass and my rhythms are now matching his. We are both in sync, and the intimacy of this moment isn't lost on either of us.

"That's it. Fuck Daddy. You are mine. You belong to me. You will never do what you did today. No more being disobedient only because you need to get fucked. This ass is so fucking tight. I'm gonna fill this ass up with cum."

"Yes please, daddy. I promise. I need it. I'm sorry. Please, please."

He yanks my hair back with a tug and pulls me close to him as his dick throbs inside of me. We look at each other and he kisses me. One arm around my body, the other around my neck as we kiss. He pulls away from the kiss.

"Daddy's about to cum. Tell Daddy where you want his cum."

"In my ass Daddy. All of it in my ass. "

He squeezes me tight like i've always loved, and thrusts so deep inside of me. It is very intense. Our breathing matches as we look in each other's eyes. I know for sure that my wrists will sport bruises but, in this moment,, I don't care. He takes one hand and reaches around and strokes my clit. He means for us to cum together it seems. Our eyes are locked in on one another. Everything is in sync. Our movements, breathing, our moving in unison like a perfect dance. I feel my release coming as I feel his too. His eyes let me know that we both are feeling the same things. I yell out first then he joins me. I feel his hard dick throbbing inside my ass as he fills my ass with his warm cum. My pussy continues to clench, and my body continues to shake, even as he pulls out of my ass. I see stars and feel weak and finally satisfied. He lets me go and I fall against the covers. He reaches over and unties my wrists. The relief is instantaneous. I am completely worn out. He lays by my side and rubs my wrists were the ropes were. I give him a soft moan as I close my eyes.

"Thank you, Daddy. That was all I needed."

Chapter 5

ELEVATOR RENDEZVOUS

The building or penthouse rather that I inherited from my grandfathers will was very classic and chic. You could tell that they had done quite a few renovations, each one better than the last. There was a doorman that let people up to their respective floors and at times escorted you inside if it was raining, or to your vehicle depending on what you needed. It was a high rise with 13 floors. I lived on the 13th floor, that I mostly had to myself. Hardly anyone could afford these penthouses, unless you came from money, won the lottery or was some sort of celebrity. Technically, I was neither of those. After my mom had passed away, I received a nice lump sum that I actually used to go back to school for interior decorating. I brought home a nice income for myself especially since it was just me. No kids and no man. My grandfather passed less than a year after I lost my mom. She was never close to him so in turn, neither was I. I was shocked that he left me anything. I never felt that he liked me. If anything, I thought that he tolerated me. I was his only grandchild. At the will reading, I was briefed on the facts. His paid off penthouse was mine, complete with all accommodations, including his parking space up front.

In addition, I also received a nice nest egg from him. He obviously saved for rainy days, that never happened. He'd lost my grandma to cancer after 40 years of marriage. I was half expecting him to donate his money to charity. I never expected anything. I got that from my mom, I guess. She worked hard all her life, and would do everything she could, so she wouldn't have to ask him for anything. I realized that while we were doing ok, before she got sick, we could have been even better if she would've put her pride to the side and accepted what he offered. But she had to be independent. That's where I got it from. Unlike her, my pride wasn't stopping me from accepting everything he left me. Thank God for my grandpa. Once I moved into the penthouse, it took me months to finish decorating and removing every trace and scent of him. He loved cigars and even if he never smoked inside, the scent was still faintly there. That meant the carpets had to go and everything had to be repainted. I was partial to hardwood floors or vinyl floors. As long as it was something that didn't hold a scent. My allergies weren't going for it. Smoke, four legged friends and shellfish were all a no go. I liked clean scents. My décor was full of pictures of horses that I'd painted with throw rugs and pillows that were beige, teal, and a splash of peach. Horses were my favorite animal. When you walked in, it felt like me, if you knew me of course. Which was exactly how I wanted it.

    I had developed a routine of sorts. I did my shopping for the week on Sundays. Depending on how I felt, I either exercised early in the morning or late in the evening. Some days I also preferred to go out, experience nature and not just go downstairs to the gym. On those particular days I would go running. Usually, come rain or shine, the doorman would greet me on my way coming and going. One particular Wednesday afternoon, as I came down to prepare to go for a run, I noticed that the usual door man wasn't there. The front desk was deserted, which was unusual. I looked around for a note of some sorts, but I found nothing. I was going to give him a few more minutes, thinking he was on his break. After about 10 minutes, I decided to go ahead and run, and I'd try to figure out the solution a little later. There was supposed to be someone available 24 hours a day. Hell, we all paid for this service. As I was putting my earbuds in, I passed this super attractive, tall, dark skinned man. His eyes had me mesmerized at first. I'm sure he thought I was a gawking weirdo. I noticed that he had on a uniform, like the workers did here. He must be new. Handsome, with pretty teeth. Goatee only, no beard, low fade, and he smelled good. Definitely my weakness. Definitely was going to stay away from him. I was taking a break from men. I was on my celibacy slash drought time. I would date men for a few months, get tired of dating and the same old bullshit, games and lies. Then I'd stop having sex and stop dating. Sometimes for a year at least. I was six months in this time. Of course, that didn't stop me from using my toys. I was still human. A woman with needs. Those needs hit differently, and more intensely after 30. Trust me.

He was still fine though. He reminded me of a taller version of Daniel from Insecure. Just not for me. I headed out the building and turned left. I felt like I was gonna push myself today, so I stopped by a bench and added more stretches than I was used to. After my muscles felt warmed up enough, I started a light jog down around the lake. It was almost 4 miles around. I was hoping to get a good time in today. I wanted to push myself more. I was switching my workouts up, hoping that would help me reach my goals faster. I had Kevin Gates song Facts playing loudly in my ears and I was in the zone that I always slip into when I'm exercising. It's almost like a meditative state. I feel my body moving, feet hitting the concrete, but couldn't tell you what I passed, or even when it started raining. By the time I made it back to the building, I definitely was soaked. My shoes were all squishy, and I could have wrung my shirt and black tights out. Good thing I had plaits in my hair piled in a bun on top of my head. I would have been pissed if I had bundles in, or a lace front on. It was a good decision to do more protective styles. I was attempting to go natural for the third time. Perhaps I'd stick to it this time. There were towels on a rack by the front desk. I grabbed two and tried to dry off as best I could. As I walked to the elevator, I could hear the squishiness of my shoes. I got on when it finally came to the lobby and rode up to my floor. It was empty, which happened occasionally, especially if they were helping another resident. I stripped as soon as my door was shut behind me. Everything was off and in a pile. I walked through the living room, feeling the cool floor and throw rugs under my feet. I looked down as I was walking. The nude color I'd picked out on my last pedicure still looked good. I had pretty feet. Every man I'd ever been with said so. I was inclined to believe them. I made it to my bathroom and started the shower. I stood in front of my mirror just admiring myself. Working out was definitely starting to show great results on my body. I grabbed my face wash off the sink and lathered my face up. I looked in my towel closet and grabbed a fresh towel and washcloth. I turned and walked to the shower. I hung the big towel on my towel rack, kept the washcloth in my hands. I tested the water first, and knew it was just how I needed it. Not hot, not cold, just enough heat so I wouldn't feel hotter than I already was. I stepped in and let the water cascade over my face. I visibly relaxed. This was always a treat. I let the water pound against my skin, especially my back. I lathered, rinsed, and relaxed a little more, then emerged from the shower about 25 minutes later. A 30-minute shower was my usual after working out. I patted myself dry and rubbed lotion into my skin. I put on my crop top from The Marathon Clothing and slipped into some ripped joggers. I wasn't planning to go anywhere today, so I saw no need for panties. I was off today and didn't want to hear a peep from my assistant about any client, so I put my phone on Do Not Disturb. They could wait until tomorrow. I headed into the kitchen, grabbed a bottle of water and some red grapes. I felt like being on the couch and was hoping to catch up on the Insecure episodes I had missed. I cut the TV on, found my throw blanket and plopped down on the recliner. Once I was comfortable, I started the episode I'd left off on. Time flew for the day, like every day off does. Soon, it was getting dark outside and I was up getting my work clothes ready and prepping my lunch for tomorrow. Once that was finished, I remembered that I hadn't checked the mail today. Which meant jumping on the elevator to go downstairs. Great.

I was looking at my phone when the elevator opened. I looked up into his eyes. Beautiful almond shaped brown eyes. It's him. His stare was piercing into mine. It made me feel like he was seeing me with no clothes on. My clit jumped and my skin was covered in chill bumps. I smiled at him, hoping what I was feeling wasn't on my face. It was hard for me to ever hide my feelings, they always showed on my face. He hit the button for the lobby. The energy between us in this space was crackling almost. I was suddenly hot, even though I didn't have on much of anything. I looked down, and my belly button piercing was shining. Stomach out, long legs glistening, nipples erect and pussy starting to get wet. I had to get out of this elevator. He looked over at me, at that precise moment and smiled. Sexy as fuck. Jeez I could melt right now.

"I'm Adonis. We saw each other earlier today."

"I recall. I'm Summer. Nice to meet you."

He stretches out his hand, and I extend mine. When our hands touch, there is a spark. More than static electricity. I feel warmth spread all over my body. We stand there looking at each other, still touching, as the elevator doors open.

"Yo, did you feel that?"

My mouth goes dry, so I lick my lips. He watches and makes it more erotic than this ever is. I let go of his hand, even though I don't want to. I miss his touch as soon as he isn't touching me anymore. What the hell does that mean?

"Yes, I definitely felt that. Let me get my mail."

I turn away quickly, but I can feel his eyes watching me. I feel like Gloria in Waiting to Exhale as I'm walking. I smile to myself. This isn't happening. I don't even know this guy. Yet I've never been this turned on by any man. The thought of fucking him passes through my mind. What in the hell was wrong with me? The thought is intriguing. I insert my key into my mailbox and pull my mail out. Half is junk and the rest are bills of course. They never stop coming. I lock my box and turn around heading back to the elevator. It's open, and he's still in the same spot as before. Waiting. His brown eyes emanating heat in my direction. I walk slowly back in the elevator. We stand there just staring at each other. Another tenant steps in, oblivious to us. He walks past me and presses the button for his floor.

"What's the point in having an employee on this thing, if I have to press my own button?"

He slowly takes his eyes off me and remembers his job.

"My apologies, Sir."

They have a polite conversation, and I've backed away from them both. I can't stop looking at him. I want the fuck outta him. We make it to the tenant's floor, and he lets him off. We ascend up two floors, when he steps forward, and touches the emergency stop button. He looks at me and I him. The energy between us seems to crackle. It's electric. We don't break eye contact. He approaches me slowly. He stops in front of me, he's not touching me, but I still feel the heat emanating from his body, and mine.

"I know this is unorthodox, and that I don't know you and you don't know me. But ever since I saw you earlier, I just wanna kiss you. Your lips are just so fucking enticing. I just gotta know if they're as soft as they look."

I say nothing. My lips part slightly, but nothing comes out. My tongue darts out of my mouth and I bite my lips slightly. It's something I do when I'm nervous. He of course doesn't know this, so it obviously makes him feel like I'm giving him the ok. He moves closer. Our noses are just inches apart. He hesitates a second, and looks in my eyes, and I nod my head. He tilts my chin up, and kisses me softly, gently.

"I knew it. They're so fucking soft."

I place my hand on his chest, which is nice and firm. I initiate the kiss this time. It's definitely not gentle or soft. It's hungry and full of need. He takes one hand and places it around my neck and pulls me even closer to him. I love being kissed like this. I feel his dick getting hard through his uniform. I can't help myself, I reach down and stroke it, through his clothes. I moan, and he moans. Then everything happens at warp speed.

The energy is heavy and we both feel it. It envelopes us like a heavy rainfall. I'm tugging at his shirt, and he's pulling my cropped top over my head. He's kissing, licking and sucking on my big brown nipples. My head is falling back and I'm giving him complete access to my breasts. He feasts on them both. But I want more, I need more. He breaks away and strips down. His dick bounces out of his boxers, and I'm stuck staring at this monster. It's not extremely long. He had to be about 5.5 inches, but the girth is what makes it a monster. It's so thick and beefy. My mouth instantly waters. I miss sucking dick. He smirks at me as he comes closer. My pussy is already waking up to the opportunity to grip some new dick. It's been so long. There are gold bars on each side of the mirrored elevator. He lifts one of my legs against the gold bar and drops to his knees. I spread my pussy lips open and he leans forward and inhales my scent. That turns me on. He puts his tongue inside of my pussy. He's making these noises as he tastes me that make me shiver all over. I'm moaning and watching him work his tongue inside me. He pulls back for a second, replacing his tongue with his finger, and he places his lips and tongue on my clit as they begin to work in unison. I'm lost in the sea of sensations that he's giving me. Each lick he gives me, he watches my reaction. It's the most erotic thing ever. I feel myself on the brink of orgasm. I make sure that he knows it.

"I'm about to cum. Please don't stop."

He watches me as I'm cumming. I lose control of my leg on the bar, but he puts that leg over his shoulder. I shake and I moan.

"Look how that pussy tightens on my fingers as you cum. Fuck."

I look down at him, as I shake and cum. When the spasms stop, he takes his finger out of me, which is coated with my cum, and he sucks the cum off his fingers. Fuck. I look down at him, lean down, and put my hands on each side of his face.

"Come here."

He gets off his knees and comes closer. I pull him closer and kiss him deep and slow. Tasting my juices on his tongue. Smelling my scent all over his face and goatee. It's sexy af. We kiss and we kiss. I murmur against him when we take a break to catch our breath.

"Please. Please fuck me."

His eyes light up, and he steps back and reaches into his pants pocket, and takes out a condom. You just happen to have a condom in your pocket? Well thank God, is what I'm thinking. His dick is so hard and pointing right at me. Momentarily, I wonder if I can take all of this dick. He'd been gentle with me so far, and I hoped he would continue. He puts the condom on and pinches the top.

"Turn around."

I eagerly turn around, arch my back and use both hands to spread my ass cheeks as I steady myself. He enters me slowly and it takes my breath away. Fuck. He gives me some of his dick, then takes it out, and puts it in again. It's literally torture and my pussy is clenching and dripping for him.

"Please."

"Please what?"

"Please fuck me. "

"Hold on to that bar. "

I brace myself as best as I could. He enters me slowly. Then he grabs my neck and fucks me. His hands are gripping my neck and ass. He's putting his entire dick in me. I'm trying to match his rhythm thrust for thrust. I'm watching him fuck me in the mirror and it's a beautiful sight. His ass is moving so fast and his thighs and balls are slapping up against me. I catch his eye in the mirror and he slaps my ass, and smiles at me. I feel my orgasm starting. I take a hand and start stroking my clit.

"That's right. Play with that pussy."

My clit stiffens, and I close my eyes. He smacks my ass hard.

"No. Look at me as you cum."

I whimper and shake. I cream all over his dick. I'm shaking, moaning, and drained looking in the mirror. He pulls me tighter to him. He goes into overdrive and I'm so depleted, I'm taking everything he gives. My pussy is gripping him tight and I can tell he loves it. He thinks I'm doing it but my pussy is doing it without me. Aftershocks of the orgasm I suppose. My ass is moving like waves crashing, with every thrust of his dick.

"Fuck. I'm about to cum."

He grips my waist tightly and is deep inside me. After a few seconds he's out of me, and I feel him cumming on my ass. It's so much of it. We both slide down to the floor. Panting, and trying to catch our breath. After a few minutes we both stand and fix our clothes. My joggers are sticking to my ass because of the cum. I'm definitely gonna have to shower again. He starts the elevator back, and we're at my floor faster than I wanted us to be. He stares at me and I him. He approaches and kisses me softly.

"Can I walk you to your door?"

I smile at him.

"Sure."

I feel his energy even as he's behind me, and I wonder if he feels my energy too. He makes me feel safe and protected. I love this feeling and I don't want it to stop. What does all of this mean, I wonder. My hand touches my doorknob, and I pause. I let my hand drop, and I look back up at him.

"Do you want to come in?"

He looks at me, and nods.

Chapter 6

Her

Every morning before work, I went into this black owned bookstore a few blocks away from my job and sat for about 30 to 45 minutes on my laptop. They also served coffee, tea, sandwiches and snacks. I never indulged. Every morning I made my own couple of cups of hot tea before heading out. I picked my flavors for the day by my mood. So, by the time I arrived, I was already wide awake and ready to start my day. I used this time to go over presentations and last-minute ideas and to use their wifi while doing it. My important before work checklist was already completed before I arrived. Prayer, meditation, a quick work out and if I had time, yoga. I was a market research analyst for BBC in downtown Atlanta. I'd been with the company for a little over a year and had established this routine months prior. Some mornings when I woke up earlier than usual, especially those nights that I couldn't sleep, I'd paint before beginning my morning ritual. The days that I was dragging in the morning and was hitting that snooze button one too many times, I'd workout in the evenings. This is something I always tried to avoid if I could. Working out always boosted my energy level and doing it later had me wired instead of sleepy at night, like I should have been.

That morning Her energy spoke to me, before she was even in my eyesight. Something said look up, so I did. I looked up at her and all I could do was stare. Our eyes met for a few seconds before we both looked away. Beautiful hazel colored eyes that seemed to twinkle when the sun caught it just so. Weirdly in that moment, it felt like some romantic comedy where everything happened in slow motion. Our maintaining eye contact seemed to last minutes when it was probably more like seconds. When I looked up again, she was seated at the table right across from me looking dead at me. We held each other's gaze for at least half a minute. Then she smiled at me and I returned that smile with one of my own. In that moment I swore I felt butterflies or some type of giddy emotion. All I could surmise was that I wasn't myself. I thought it was the best time to introduce myself. If I wouldn't have, later I would've reflected back on how rude that would have been.

"Hi, I'm Monáe."

"I'm Aaliyah, and it's nice to meet you."

"You as well. Is it spelled like the late singer/actor Aaliyah?"

"It is yes."

I couldn't help but stare at her. She was so beautiful. Her skin glowed, like it was a light underneath her skin. Like the sun itself had kissed her or lit a fire inside. Her lips were a beautiful shade of brown. She had on clear gloss and her lips looked so soft. She was the color of mahogany. That's the best way I could describe it. It fit her perfectly. She had long small plaits that came to her butt. She couldn't have gotten them too long ago because they still looked freshly done. And the tattoos. She had so many tattoos that were visible. Her hands and her wrists looked like henna tattoos. Her neck had small birds seemingly in a small flock. It disappeared into her lavender colored shirt. It made me wonder if she had more, in places that couldn't be seen. The thought of that had me blushing hard. Observing her, our complexions weren't too different. I was perhaps a couple shades lighter. Not that it mattered. I loved how my skin looked draped in deep purples, blues, golds and greens. I always felt majestic and royal in those colors. Like a queen. She'd be stunning in those colors too. Perfect even. I tried to stop staring, but it was hard not to. I bet our skin right next to each other, would be quite a sight to see. She and I were different in other ways though. I had no tattoos and I was wearing my naturally 4c hair in a high bun. My baby hairs were behaving today. I loved gold more than any other type jewelry at the moment. I also loved simplicity. I had a pair of gold hoop earrings on with a gold bracelet and anklet. She had on 3 necklaces, 3 silver earrings on each ear and about 5 silver bracelets on each arm. I was tall. 5'10" to be exact. She had to be 5'3". Not that it mattered to me. It actually made me more attracted to her. I had no idea if she was feeling the same or if she was being polite and simply tolerating me. Hell, I didn't know her sexuality and I felt it rude to ask on our first encounter. I was basically pansexual and more attracted to energy than a certain sex. She kept smiling this slow languid smile at me. To be completely honest, it was actually turning me on.

I was feeling spontaneous and I figured, what the hell. I should just go ahead and jump out the window and ask this beautiful goddess out. But unfortunately, glancing down at my watch, I needed to head out. I smiled at her, told her it was nice to meet her and left. My workday went by fast. I won't deny that I had moments where I would daydream to thoughts of her. I scolded myself for acting like a schoolgirl with a crush. Once I was walking out the building, I was trying to decide what my night was going to be like. It was Friday after all and I was ready for the weekend. I'd been thinking about checking out a new club downtown that had just opened, The Broadway. Supposedly it was always packed with a mixed crowd. Mixed as in gays and straights were welcome there. I'd overheard a few coworkers talking about it. During the week they had karaoke and poetry night. It was also a mostly black crowd but of course, any race was welcome. Definitely my kind of bar. I decided as I was walking home that I'd check it out tonight. I turned the key, walked inside my 2-bedroom apartment, greeted Max my Rottweiler and headed to the bathroom. As I stripped off my clothes and started my bath water, she popped into my head. I wondered if she was the type to frequent clubs. Honestly, I really wasn't the type. I literally went out every blue moon and even then, I never stayed long. I was adding oil and bath bombs and roses to my claw foot tub. It had been a long day and I needed to relax. The bad thing is, when I did this, I usually was so drained when I got out, I'd hop in pajamas. We'll see if tonight was any different. I put my fingers in the water and it was just perfect. I got in and put my neck back and relaxed. My muscles immediately sighed with relief. Next Lifetime was playing softly through my Bluetooth that I had connected to the speakers I had around the place. My thoughts started wandering to her again. Her eyes, her lips and the way they moved. Her name and the way she looked at me. My hands were caressing my breasts before I knew it. I was pulling my nipples and encircling my thumbs over them. Replaying our encounter had my pussy throbbing. I let one of my breasts go, and slowly started touching my body. I let go of my other breast and started rubbing my stomach and hips and thighs. I took two fingers from my right hand and put them on my pussy. I took my left hand and held my pussy lips open and started rubbing my clit slowly. A soft moan escaped my lips and I would alternate putting my fingers inside my pussy and rubbing my clit. I was so into it I was moaning louder than the music playing. I had to stop holding my pussy open so I could rub my clit fast and use the other hand to penetrate my pussy more. I felt the sensation of an orgasm about to wash over me. Just as it was about to overtake me, Max came crashing into the bathroom, barking at me and scared the fuck out of me. Great. I should have walked him soon as I got home. On the flip side, I wasn't drained and had plenty energy. I guess I was going out after all.

I Uber there because I don't want to be drinking and driving tonight and I wanted to enjoy myself. The line is around the building when I get dropped off. Luckily, it's moving quickly. I'm in the building in about 15 minutes. The first place I go to is the bathroom. I'd stepped outside of my comfort zone and chose to wear this fuchsia short dress. The back was out somewhat. Right down the middle, like someone ripped it, and clipped it back together. It felt like silk against my skin. I'd redone my bun over. I added some cute lil baby hairs and looking in the mirror, a few coils of my hair had gotten free. It was cute though, so I left it that way. I'd chosen these cute nude stilettos that had cute lil straps that went up the leg. Once I'd finished in the bathroom, I headed to the bar. Summer Walker's Girls Need Love Remix with Drake is playing loud and I'm ready to get my drink on. After waiting 10 minutes to get the bartenders attention, I have my Dusse on the rocks. I'm sipping slow and surveying the crowd. I'm also trying to decide if I wanna hang by the bar or start trying to find somewhere to sit or if I just want to dance. The DJ puts on Heat by Chris Brown. That made the decision for me. I hurriedly finished my drink and headed to the dance floor. The bass is so heavy on this dance floor that I can literally feel it. I'm dancing alone and I have my hands up, two stepping with the beat and I feel someone come up behind me. I immediately stop moving, not knowing who it is. Hoping it isn't some creep, I turn to face them, and it's her. She's wearing this soft looking olive-green jumpsuit with no bra. She has silver pasties covering her nipples, that make me wonder what they look like. She has her hair up in a bun too and she looks delectable. She leans towards me and says *"Don't stop dancing. I liked watching you."*

That somewhat embarrasses me, but I relax and start moving again. With her heels on, she's not far from my original height. This time as I move to the beat, she joins me, and we have a cute lil two step going on. We dance for 2 songs straight. After the last song I smile at her and head towards the bar. The buzz I thought I had is gone and I need another drink or 2. She's at my side and she smiles at me.

"I was wondering if I'd see you again. Good thing I decided to come out tonight."

Wow. My thoughts are racing now because we were both thinking the same thing.

"What did you order?" she asks.

"A double shot of Dusse."

She looks at me, and the bartender comes back with my drink. She smiles at me.

"Follow me."

I put a $20 on the bar and follow her. Whatever scent she's wearing is intoxicating. We make our way through the crowd and we come upon this table. It has a big bottle of Dusse there, a bucket of ice, with cups.

"You got a table for yourself?"

"Yeah, I don't care for people that much. I wanted my own area."

We sit beside each other, and she pours herself a drink, and adds ice. I sip mine quickly and she pours me more. She keeps staring in my eyes and I don't look away at all. The music is blasting around us, and the crowd is getting bigger. There is a commotion on the dance floor, and she leans over and asks me if I wanna go.

"But we haven't finished the bottle."

She laughs, and says we'll take it with us. She leads us out of the club. As soon as we make it out of the side entrance, it's raining outside.

"I live just up the block. Do you wanna get an Uber or make a run for it?"

I look at her and I just know I want her. Now. I look in her eyes. She looks in mine. I take two steps towards her, and my lips part. She smiles at me, and that's the confirmation I need. I take another step and touch her face softly. We both come closer, and my lips are on hers and we kiss softly. Her lips are soft, and her tongue is sweet. I have a hand on both sides of her face. I pull her closer to me and deepen the kiss. When we finally pull away from each other, we realize that we're standing here getting wet, in more ways than one.

"Let's make a run for it", she says.

She grabs my hand and we jog a couple blocks. We're at her door in minutes, and we're definitely soaking wet.

"I'm gonna get us some towels. Wait right here."

I start coming out of my wet clothes when she leaves. By the time she's back, I'm completely naked. She looks at me and licks her lips. I smile at her. She hands me a fluffy gray towel. I start drying off while she strips out of her clothes. She dries off and we're both standing there naked. She rushes to me and I meet her halfway. My lips are on hers and we're touching each other slowly. Her mouth is so wet and warm. I start kissing her neck and rubbing her breasts. She has a beautiful ankh tattoo between her breasts. She pulls the pasties off slowly, and I see her nipples are pierced. Both have small silver hoops. Her breasts are perfect. Just about a C cup, standing at attention. I feel like I'm towering over her with our shoes off. She looks at me like she understands what I'm thinking. She pushes me towards her couch. She sits in my lap, and we kiss, and we kiss before we both take our hair down and start kissing again. She takes her hand and cuffs my left breasts.

"These are perfect."

I laugh. *"These big ol thangs? I think yours are absolutely perfect."*

She goes from breast to breast, caressing, sucking and rubbing. I'm rubbing her back softly and we're both moaning. She scoots off my lap and sits in front of me. Not completely on her knees, but it's like she's sitting off to the side. She stares at my pussy, and she just looks at me with so much desire. I lean forward to kiss her and she pushes me back. Her soft hands rub my bare pussy slowly. She puts her face between my legs, and I feel her breathing and hear her inhaling. She pulls me forward a little and I raise both of my legs up and scoot farther towards the edge of the sofa. She starts licking my pussy slowly. She leaves no spot untouched, untasted or unlicked. One of my hands is in her hair as she's tasting me while the other is caressing my nipples.

"This pussy tastes so good."

I can't even respond, all I can do is moan. This is so much different than being with a man. She takes pride in her work. She is attentive. She's not in any rush. She wants to make sure I am pleased thoroughly. This doesn't go on for seconds, it goes on for many minutes. She made me cum hard when she put one finger inside me and sucked softly on my clit. Then she began slowly tongue fucking my pussy and lapping up every taste of cream. I reach for her, because I want to return the favor, but she doesn't let me.

"I'm not finished yet."

I let her have her way with me. I was gonna patiently wait my turn because I needed her lil ass to ride my face. There is no need for toys or straps or anything. Her soft pink tongue and her fingers are all I need. She's gaining speed sucking on my clit. She adds another finger inside me and starts finger fucking me fast. My body locks up and I squirt without being able to warn her. She didn't move. She smiles at me, face dripping and her licking her lips. I come close to her and kiss her passionately. She feeds me her fingers. I feast on her tongue and her breasts. She goes to sit down, and I stop her.

"Sit on my face."

She looks at me in a knowing way. I lay down on the floor and she comes and squats over me. She has a pretty pussy, big clit that's landscaped. As it gets closer to my face, her aroma is addictive and her pussy is already bubbling wet. I put one of my fingers inside her as soon as she's comfortable. I lick every crevice and leave nothing untouched. She's riding my face like a seat. I latch on to her clit softly and suck it.

"Fuck baby yes. Don't stop. Eat that pussy."

I take my time bringing her to climax. I get her almost there, then I back off of the pressure.

"Don't tease me. Let me cum in your mouth."

Just hearing her say that makes me want to know what her cum tastes like. I give her the pressure she needs. She reaches down, grabs my hair and positions my head just so. It's kind of uncomfortable in this position, but I'll take it to ensure her pleasure. After a few more minutes, I have my prize.

"Fuck. Omg I'm about to cum. Don't stop. Don't stop."

She creams on my face, as I continue to suck her clit. When she starts inhaling quickly, I back up off her clit and put my tongue deep inside her. She lets me have my fun but after a little while, she's at her limit.

"Baby I can't take anymore."

She slowly climbs off my face and just lays there.

"You wanna get into the bed?"

"Mmmhmmm. Give me like 5 minutes."

We both laugh. We lay in silence for a few minutes, and it feels normal, and not awkward at all.

"I'm glad we were on the same page. I wasn't sure if you were into women."

"I'm into a lot of things. I don't know why you couldn't tell. I was trying to throw it at you after that first smile."

We both laughed.

"No but for real. I haven't had fun like this in awhile. I needed this."

"What's awhile?"

"Probably about 8 months ago."

"What about you?"

"Probably 2 years."

"Damn why so long?"

"Getting over a breakup."

"Oh I get it. That can be hard sometimes. Can you join me in bed and *stay awhile, or do you have to go?"*

"I can stay. I'm in no rush to run back out in the rain, and jump in an Uber."

She stands up, and motions for me to follow her. I walk behind her, and notice more tattoos. They look like Chinese letters all down her spine. They're all so sexy on her. She has a platform bed that's up high. I love it, but I'm wondering how she jumps in bed every night. She looks at me, and smiles.

"Don't be judging me. I have a stool by the bed. I like high beds."

"So do I. It's much better than sleeping in a bed close to the floor. I've done that, and I don't recommend it for anyone."

Looking around, her room is so clean. Like ocd clean. I'm sporting her cum on my face, and my cum on my thighs. I hesitate before touching her bed.

"You mind if I shower?"

"No not at all. Everything you need is in the bathroom closet."

"Thanks."

I head in there, but I don't close the door at all. I see a clip on her sink that i'm thankful for, because my hair tie is still in her living room. I put my hair up, turn the water on and go searching for a towel and washcloth in the closet. I find them easily, but I also notice male and female products in here. Not that it means anything. Sometimes I like the scent of a man's cologne on my skin. I tell myself that's what it is and head to the shower. We didn't have a conversation about our lives or what we want or where this is going. We owe each other nothing. I'm just gonna enjoy the ride.

My face was directly in the spray as I let the water cascade down on me. I felt her before she even touched me. She was behind me, touching me, stroking me, as I'm soaping up my towel. We switch places and I soap up my entire body as she rinses off. She's even more beautiful as the water cascades down her body. I'm in awe of her. We switch places again and I rinse off as she soaps up. I'm finished first so I step out of the shower to towel off. She joins me minutes later. We're both admiring each other's body as we oil down. I walk naked into her bedroom and she follows. She stops me as I reach the bottom of the bed.

"Wait. Don't move. Stay just like that."

My back is to her and she's behind me. She bends me over and tells me to place my hands on the bed. I feel like I'm being frisked by the cops. But this is so much better. Her tongue is slowly licking and tasting me from behind. I spread my legs even wider to accommodate her. She's up under me now, sucking my clit and fingering my pussy. Now it's my turn to ride her face. I worry about putting too much of my weight on her but she's literally pulling me closer to her face. She won't let me be gentle with her. She wants to feel my pressure.

"Ride my fucking face, and stop playing with me."

She slaps my ass hard, and I forget all about her size compared to mine. I start riding her pretty face preparing to cum all on it.

"That's it. Ride my face, cum in my mouth sexy."

I plan to do just that. I reach down and grab her braids and hold her in the exact position I need her in.

"Don't you fucking stop. Stay right there, right fucking there. "

She does just as I ask and the cum sprays out of me and this time she's prepared. I hear her gulping and sucking and moaning, telling me how good I taste. She drains me well and I feel more satisfied than I have in years. I collapse face down on the bed, ass still in the air. I hear her open and close her chest of drawers. I hear something being opened and maybe squeezed out. I'm laying there anticipating her next move. She slides the strap in me slowly, and all I can do is moan and shiver.

"This is what you wanted right?"

"Yes. Please, fuck me."

Her strokes are everything I need them to be. Slow and deep. My pussy clenches the strap and won't let go.

"Look how that pussy grips the dick."

I'm moaning and attempting to throw it back on her, but her little ass is fucking the shit out of me. Truthfully I hold on to the covers tightly, and embrace the ride. No woman has ever fucked me like this. How did someone so petite have this much in them? She definitely wasn't a novice at all. She pulls my hair and slaps my ass.

"Yes, don't stop, make me cum on the dick."

She seemingly flips a switch, and goes into overdrive. I'm literally holding on for dear life.

"Look how that ass moves."

She keeps smacking both cheeks, and I feel myself coiling tight like a spring. It won't be long now.

"Come for me sexy."

That's all I need to hear. I don't cum as hard this time and I don't squirt. I cream all over the strap and my body continues to shake even after I've finished cumming. I lay my body down completely flat on her bed. She joins me and asks me to get under the covers with her. She is the big spoon and I'm the little one. In minutes we're both knocked out. A few hours later, she's shaking me awake.

"You have to get dressed, you have to go."

"Why what's the urgency, what's wrong?"

"My husband is back from his trip early, and I don't want him to catch you here."

I look at her, and I know I have the saddest look ever.

"Your husband??"

Chapter 7

Not in the mood

Lauryn: *"Are you going to tell me what's wrong, or do I have to suck it out of you?"*

That makes him look up from his phone. He hasn't said two words to me since he came home. I heard his truck pull up and I was in the utility room doing laundry when he'd walked right past me without saying anything. No kiss, no hug, nothing. That wasn't like him at all. I had finished the clothes, cleaned the kitchen and had just gotten out of the shower and he still hadn't said a word to me. He was in bed with his pajama bottoms on only. Black has always been a tall big dude. 6'4", dark skin, a little bit of a belly and a beard that I loved so much. Dark brown piercing eyes and swole arms covered in tattoos. My teddy bear. One thing I've always loved was his size but there were times that I knew it made him self conscious and maybe even insecure. I don't know why though, he was perfect to me. Yet, his focus was that damn phone. Every night it was the same thing. At least 12 to 16 hours of the day he was gone driving trucks, yet when he came home, it was quiet, it was no love, no kissing, no touching, no heat, just coldness. I had had enough.

"Say what? What you said?"

"You heard me, what's it gonna be?"

He gets quiet. But he does put the phone down, which is rare. He kinda stares off to the side instead of looking at me. So, this nigga wasn't gonna answer me? Ok cool. Fine. Say less. I take my silk robe off and pull the covers back.

"What are you doing?"

"Exactly what I said. I'm going to suck it out of you."

"Man stop playing man. I'm tired."

"Who's playing? You acting like you don't want me to Black!"

"I just wanna relax. It's been a long day, and I'm not in the mood tonight. That's all I'm saying."

"You not in the mood? What kind of fuck shit? You ain't never turned me down black. What your dick tired from you fucking around or what?"

"Man come on, don't start that bs. I'm not cheating on your crazy ass. A nigga can't be tired sometimes? Gotdamn, I'm working 80 plus hour weeks, I don't hang out with the fellas, I come home to yo ass, I'm paying all these bills. Can a nigga get a break sometimes?"

A break? All I've been giving his ass is a break. I knew something was up, but I never wanted to fight. I'd been silent about this for weeks now, but I couldn't take it anymore.

"Fine Black, if that's what you want."

I put my robe back on and tighten it around my waist as I walk out of the bedroom and head to the kitchen to pour me some wine. I flipped the TV on and was trying to find something interesting to watch. I gave up after 30 minutes. It never fails. I was on my second glass of wine when I figured he'd be sleeping now anyway. I gulp that down and feeling quite buzzed now, I head back to our bedroom. I go into our closet and find my box of toys. I'm searching for my quiet clit sucker. I'd tried so many Adam and Eve products, they should be paying me to test them out. I make sure that bad boy has a full charge. I come out the closet and find my headphones. I look over at him and his phone is on the charger and just like I thought, he's knocked out. I climb up into bed and go through my bookmarked porn. I find the one that reminds me of Black and I about 5 years ago. He's coming in from work, kissing me, and touching on me and turning me on. Him letting me suck his dick all sloppy while he talked to me nasty. Him slapping my ass and grabbing my hair and fucking me deeply and telling me how much he missed my pussy and mouth today. The memories were taking over for the porn. I had my eyes closed tightly, with the toy close against my clit. It really felt like a mouth. Sucking and blowing against my clit. I'm trying to be as quiet as I can but it's so fucking good. My legs are open, and one hand is holding the toy, and the other has dropped the phone and I'm stroking my breast. I believe I'm being quiet enough, because Black hasn't moved. I feel like I'm gonna cum soon and I just hope I can stay quiet.

Black: I loved the hell out of my wife. I'd never cheat on her crazy ass. Things were just not how they used to be. She still looked good, but I had put on some pounds. She was tall, brown skin, almond shaped seductive eyes, big breasts, (I was a breast man), with the softest skin. She was perfect for me. She used to beg me for it but now if we fucked twice a week, that was a lot. That's all it was too, monotonous fucking. I missed that freaky shit. I was starting to feel like I wasn't enough for her. My dick wasn't small, but over this belly, maybe it wasn't the size I once thought it was. Sometimes my dick would get hard but not stay hard. I had to spend more time on foreplay or else I wasn't lasting long like I used to. I know she watches porn, and I knew she had a duffel bag full of them damn toys that she thought I didn't know she uses a lot more often now. Yeah, I'm on my phone more, looking at IG girls, remembering what I used to be capable of. I wouldn't cheat on Lauryn, but sometimes the fantasy is there. I didn't want to keep giving her quickies and her just accepting that shit. I was thinking maybe I'd try Viagra, or some of the fellas at my job had been talking about these pills in the convenience stores. I just wanted to please my wife again. Make her crave me like she used to. Wear that good pussy out. Quiet as kept, I shouldn't have turned down that head. One of the reasons I married her was her head. Like nigga. She was gifted.

I was deep in my dream of getting a new deck on the back, when I hear her moaning. She watching that damn porn I know it. I look over at her, and her eyes are shut. She not watching no porn. Her phone is facedown, and her earphones are out. It's obvious she trying to be quiet, but I can hear her. I get still and I listen to her. She saying my name over and over. Damn. This whole time I thought my baby wanted someone else but she still want me. Even after putting on weight and cumming too fast and not staying hard, she still wants me. It makes my heart warm knowing that. I definitely married the right woman. I been showing my fucking ass. Let me make this shit up to her. I don't wanna lose her to someone else. I feel her shaking hard. She gonna cum any second now. She so into it, she doesn't feel me moving in the bed. I move the toy away just in time and I catch her cum all in my beard. She's still moaning my name with her eyes closed. I put two fingers inside her pussy and start lapping her pussy up slowly. She is always sensitive for a few minutes after she cums, so I was letting her body relax before I took her clit in my mouth. She finally opens her eyes and looks down at me.

"Damn Black, I needed you so bad baby, thank you."

I'm moaning as I lick her, and I watch her come out of that silk robe completely. She's stroking and rubbing her nipples and moaning looking at me.

"I love you so much baby."

I love you too I try to say with my mouth full. I test the clit out and she rubs my head, letting me know it's ok to suck it and I suck on that pretty rosebud lookin clit so softly. Then I lick it and I put more pressure behind my sucks. I wanna do better than that damn toy. I'm moaning and sucking because she likes that.

"Yes Black, omg don't stop. Right there. Right there."

She holds my head tightly in that spot, and I'm still fingering that wet pussy. I start curving my fingers inside of her. If a camera was inside her pussy, it would look like I was saying come here.

"Spit on it Black, spit on that pussy and slurp it back up."

She loves that. I give her just what she needs.

"Fuuuckkkkk."

She's holding my head, and has tilted her pelvis up, and is definitely putting that sweet pussy in my face. I'm enjoying the ride, and I know I'll have my prize soon.

"Black! Black!"

"Yes baby", I say between breaths.

"I'm gonna cum. You're gonna make me squirt all over your face babe!"

"Do it, give it all to me."

As soon as her legs clamp down on me, I suck her clit three more times, then I put my face where my fingers were. She squirts out like a hose. Her legs are up, and I'm gulping down her juices, and she's sucking her pussy juice off my fingers. Her body still spasms as I keep licking slowly, even after swallowing all her greatness. I come up over her and my beard is dripping her juices on her. She opens her legs wider and pulls me on top of her. She kisses me slow and deep, sucking her juice off my tongue and inhaling her scent in my beard.

"Damn I smell so good and taste so good."

"Damn right you do, I love that sweet pussy."

We're kissing slowly and she's rubbing me, and my insecurities try to pop back up in my head, and she looks at me.

"Make love to me Black. I need you."

I'd swear she has tears in her eyes, and it does something to me. I don't care about anything but pleasing this woman. Seeing her want me this bad is what I needed. My dick is rock hard, and I slowly guide it inside my baby. My dick knows exactly what she needs. Her legs are around my back, pushing me deeper inside her. I look down at her and tears are coming out of her eyes.

"Baby?"

"No don't stop baby, keep going please."

I cradle her head and look in her eyes. I lean down and kiss her tears. She pulls me to her mouth, and we keep kissing for what seems like forever. She usually likes to swallow my cum, but when I feel it coming, she pulls me closer, and opens her legs wide. It feels so good to cum inside of this wet warm pussy. I'm breathing heavy, and she's stroking my back. I feel my heavy load pulse out my dick, and I bury it deep inside her. I'm so drained when I'm finished, and I really can't move.

"Stay like this baby, don't move she says. Sleep with your dick still inside me."

I move my body so I'm still inside her, but she's able to breathe. She rubs my head gently and we both fall asleep.

Lauryn: We wake up that next morning, and I know that something is different. Something has changed between us. Last night was special.

Your dick is soft inside of me at first, but as you begin to wake up, it gets rock hard. You're definitely feeling heavy on top of me. But I like it. I feel like you're my shield, my protection. You open your eyes, and I hug you tight. You put your lips against my neck, and you tell me you love me. You start moving slowly inside me. My pussy is now awake too. You make love to me so softly, and it feels so good. Every stroke you give me, is matched with my thrusting against you. After a few minutes, you tell me to hold my legs up. I open my legs wide, and you kiss me softly. Morning breath and all. I feel your dick throbbing deep inside me.

"Tell me where you want me to cum baby."

"Deep inside me, Black. Deep inside baby.

I feel your cum squirting inside me, and after you've given me every drop, you relax your body, and I feel all your weight on me.

"Baby, I can't breathe."

We both laugh, you go up on your arms, kiss me and pull out of me, lying beside me.

"Thank you for giving me what I needed Black. I know things have been strained between us, but I need more of you."

"I know baby. I'm sorry I've been distant. I will be better. I love you and don't want anyone but you."

"You saying that is all I needed to hear babe. It quiets my fears and insecurities. It makes me want you even more."

8 weeks go by, and things are so much better between Black and I. It reminds me of how it used to be. Until that one day when you walk in on me, while I'm in the bathroom.

"Lauryn, is that what I think it is?"

"Yes..."

"What does it say?"

"It says that I'm pregnant"

"You sure?"

"Yes Black. I'm sure. This is my third test."

You run to me and pick me up in the air.

"I'm gonna be a father!!!"

Chapter 8

MARRIED MAN

We became Facebook friends by happenstance. I didn't know you and you didn't know me. We lived in the same town, so why not hit accept? You caught my eye by your height. You seemed to be the tallest one in your photos. You told me you were 6'5". I was thrilled, because I loved tall men. I wasn't short by any standards. 5'9" for a woman definitely wasn't short. You were bald, like shiny bald, with a baby face that had no facial hair when I met you. Pretty white smile. Long thick fingers, manicured hands. Dark-skin with a medium build, if I was going by your pictures. I wasn't dark and I wasn't light. I still was very much a black female, regardless. I weighed close to 190, with DD size breasts. The usual prerequisite, pretty face, nice lips, curvy, plus size. blah blah. You had these beautiful big dark lips. They looked so soft on your pictures. We began having conversations when I was online, through messenger. We eventually exchanged numbers, just to reach each other faster.

I was with my boyfriend at the time, and you were with your girlfriend at the time. It was all very innocent at first. The attraction was there of course, but we never spoke on trying to pursue it. If anything, it was a definite friendly vibe. We confided in each other, we talked for hours on the phone. I complained about him and you complained about her. We talked about our kids, and we spoke of our goals, and where we wanted to be in a years time. We agreed to meet one night. Just a quick meet and greet on your way home from work. Headed to her. You were working as a selector at the time for some warehouse. We met not far from my apartment. I chose a feed store that I knew would be deserted at that time of night. I pulled up in my car and you pulled up in your truck. We basically hop out at the same time.

"Wow you're really handsome. And definitely tall. You make me feel short. That's rare."

We both laughed.

"You're beautiful. You look exactly like your pictures. That's rare too."

We stared at each other for what felt like minutes. Smiling and staring.

"Well I should go. I just wanted to finally meet you. Can I have a hug?"

That hug seemed to last longer than a regular hug should've. I didn't want to let go and neither did you. You smelled so good. It was definitely expensive cologne. I could just tell.

"I'll hit you up later ok?"

"Alright, drive safe."

We both got in our vehicles and drove away. I got home and thought about you all night. When my boyfriend came home and wanted sex, I jumped on top, and reverse cowgirled, so I wouldn't face him. I imagined that it was you I was on top of. I really got into it, on my feet, then my toes, giving it my all. I came so hard that night and so did he. Unaware that I was fucking another man in my head.

We continued to have conversations all the time. You were gonna be off a day during the week, and wanted to meet at a park, before the sun went down, just to walk around the lake and talk. Friend with another friend.

We met up around the same time. I parked not far from you. We caught each other's eyes. We walked to meet each other and hugged. It still felt like it had the other night. It felt right. We walked around the park/lake one time, and it started to drizzle and looking up at the sky, it wasn't gonna stop anytime soon. We headed towards our cars. We got to yours first, and mine was not far in the opposite direction. You stopped me from moving.

"Stay. Don't go yet. I got time. We can sit in my car and talk, if that's ok. If you don't have anywhere to go. If he won't be missing you yet."

I looked at my phone.

"I've got time."

You unlocked your doors, and we hopped in your truck, out of the rain. You stared at me and I you.

"Thanks."

"For what?"

"For staying. I needed you to."

Your eyes got this sadness to them that I didn't like. Something was wrong. You started telling me about your mother and your father. How they weren't great parents and how your relationship was strained. We talked, and we talked. Easily an hour passed. It felt like minutes. It always did between us. That was nothing new. At some point in the conversation, you looked at me, and I you. The energy changed at that moment. I could feel it, and I know you could too.

"Come here."

I leaned in closer to you. You looked in my eyes and you closed yours and kept moving closer. You were gonna kiss me. I wanted this and had secretly thought about it for a while. Once our lips touched, that was it. My soft lips against your soft lips was everything. Your tongue on mine, sucking softly, had me so turned on. My pussy was getting wet and from feeling your body as we kissed, your dick was getting hard. But tonight, it just wasn't the night for us to go all the way. You meant something to me, and I just didn't want to fuck you so soon. Many other meet ups occurred after that, and we would talk, kiss, and lose track of time. One night you asked me to meet you at the park. It was on the outskirts of town, where we wouldn't be seen. It was the more affluent part of town and we figured we would be safe. It was deserted at that time of night, but we could see cars passing by. Lights flashing, but no one turning in. We both were out of our vehicles, and up against my car just talking and laughing. You kissed me mid laugh, and then the kiss became hungrier than any other kiss. It didn't matter that it wasn't completely dark. It didn't matter that cars were passing by. The lights were shining on us from every turn, that each car made. It didn't matter that we were outside, and could be seen by anyone. We were focusing on the below the waist clothes. Your sweats came down, and your black cotton boxer briefs. My ripped camo pants came off, and my black lace boy shorts. You pushed me back on the hood of my car and spread my legs. It was like a roller coaster ride that I was trying my best to hold on to. You were fingering slowly and sucking and licking all over my pussy. You spread my lips like a beautiful rose being opened up. I was moaning your name and rubbing your head. The more you fingered me while tasting me, the more I knew I was gonna cum hard and squirt everywhere. You didn't even know I could squirt. We hadn't had conversations like that yet. To be honest, I was still embarrassed about it. But I couldn't control it. You were going to find out today. Your fingers seemed to be in overdrive and your tongue was applying just the right amount of pressure. It happened. My pussy clamped tight around your fingers, my clit swelled, and I released squirt everywhere, and you weren't fazed by it at all. You lifted your shirt, and you pulled me close to you. My ass was partly hanging off my cars hood. You swiftly put a condom on and entered me fast. We both exhaled.

"Damn this pussy was worth the fucking wait. You got that wet wet baby. "

I'm moaning, and you're groaning. We hear a car horn that's not too far. We both look at each other, remembering that we are outside in a public park. We don't stop, but we put a rush on things, not wanting to get caught. My legs are around you tight and you're trying to be gentle but find yourself distracted by the warmth and grip. You start going faster and a little deeper. You don't want to hurt me by giving me the entire dick. You definitely were the biggest dick I'd ever had, and I was busy trying to accommodate your size and throw this pussy back on you. After five or six strokes, the sweat was dripping off your forehead thanks to this Florida humidity and your dick seemed to get even harder. I knew it wouldn't be long until you were ready to cum.

"Please babe let me swallow it. Please."

You looked me in my eyes, and yours seemed to shine. You gave me two more deep strokes, and then pulled out and quickly pulled off the condom. I took you in my mouth, sucked hard, and pulled with all the suction gusto I could. You filled my throat with your cum and braced yourself with one hand. I kept sucking but much softer than before. I sucked until your dick was a mere fraction of what it was a minute ago. You stroked the side of my face, leaned down, and kissed my forehead.

"Come on, let's go."

We both put our clothes back on and pulled them up. My legs were shaking as I walked to the driver side of my car. You were in your truck and had turned your car and headlights on.

"Call me when you get home, so I know you made it safe."

I told you that I would, and you waited until I was heading out the park first then you came behind me. I was headed left, and you were headed right. At this time, we lived on opposite sides of town. Once home,

I texted you that I made it home safe. You texted back that you needed to see me again soon. You said you wouldn't be able to go long without more. That was a Thursday. I knew I'd probably hear from you by the weekend, but I didn't. I had texted you a couple times, but you'd left me on read. Saturday night you texted me that we'd have to meet up next Thursday again. You said you were going out of town for a few days and would hit me up when you came back. That was odd to me. You always talked to me no matter where you were and what was up. I wasn't gonna trip off of it, but in the back of my mind, I knew you weren't being honest about something. I pushed that thought back and kept on like it was nothing. Monday evening once I got home and the kids were outside playing and my boyfriend at the time was across town, I texted you. You left me on read for an hour, then texted me that you'd call me in a few minutes. Something was definitely up. I went on Facebook and was scrolling my timeline. Not even 15 seconds had passed, and you were on my timeline in a tux, and she was in a wedding dress. I quickly went to your page and went through all the pictures and comments. So you married her?

I was still reading comments when my phone started ringing and it was you.

"Hey sorry I haven't been available to see you."

"Were you never gonna tell me? You'd rather me find out through Facebook??"

"I didn't plan for you to find out that way. She put the pics up and tagged me in them and didn't even speak to me about it."

"So why are you even calling me?"

"Shit this won't change what you and I share. I'm not letting you go because of this ring."

I put my phone down and just stared at it. You kept calling my name.

"Bianca. Bianca."

I pressed End. The tears were running down my face. I couldn't be mad at you. We were both in relationships from the beginning. But in my mind, I was going to leave him for you. That's what I wanted. But of course, you never knew that. I never had time to tell you. Married. Yet you wanted to continue. Fuck it. It was time I let you go. I blocked you. From Facebook, Instagram, and on my phone. It was like we never even happened. Even though we both know that it did.

A year passed. I broke up with my boyfriend. I'd moved to your side of town, but I had no idea if you still lived this way or not. Being a married man and all, maybe your wife wanted to be somewhere different. Months went by, and I thought I had put you out of my mind. I was wrong. One night I couldn't sleep, and I tossed and turned. I got out of bed at like 2am, and my daughter was still up. I asked her if she wanted to go to Walmart with me. Once there, I didn't want to get out. I handed her my list of a few items to her and told her to get what she wanted. Off she went. About 10 minutes had passed by, and I was alternating being on my phone and watching the customers come and go. One particular customer came out with a big bag of dog food, balanced on his shoulders. His walk looked eerily familiar. He was coming down the same lane I was parked on. He had a beard, but those eyes were unmistakable. It was you. I stared at you and slunk down in my seat a little. I wasn't dressed and my hair wasn't done. It didn't matter anyway. You never looked in my direction. I never went to sleep that night. I tossed and turned. Around 11am, I gave up, and got ready for the day. I was off but I still had errands to run. As the day progressed, it kept gnawing at me to unblock you. It wasn't like you'd get a notification that I did. So, I did. I went on your page and went through all the posts and pictures you had that were open to the public. Plenty of things weren't being shown and I was itching to see what they were. The next few hours I debated on sending you a friend request. Eventually I did. Five minutes didn't even pass, and you accepted it. I poured over everything. Your wife was cute, but she wasn't me. Seeing pictures of y'all together had me asking why her? I was gonna leave my ex for you and move you in with the two kids I had from him. I kept looking over everything. I eventually lurked hard enough until I was on her page. Of course, she tagged you in everything. She obviously loved you. No way I believed you loved her like that, but what did it matter now? You married her. So that was that I guess. Until you messaged me.

"Finally. I've been missing the fuck out of you baby. I need to see you."

In my mind, I wanted to cuss your fuck ass out. I wanted to scream and cry. Yet instead.

"When?"

"Later tonight, round 12. That's cool? Meet me at the dark area at the mall where it's real dark."

"Ok."

"You're not gonna flake and block me again are you?"

"No, I'll be there."

I should have put on clown makeup and clown shoes because that's exactly how I fucking felt. Yet my heart was crying out for you, and my pussy was begging to have more of that dick. I wasn't ready to let you go yet.

The hours go by so fast of course. I'm waiting in my car with air on high, playing Ashanti low, lost in thought. You tap my window before I knew it. I roll my window down and you tell me to get out. I roll my window up and turn my car off. I get out and just look up at you. You rush to me, kiss me while holding me tight. For some reason, after about 3 minutes, I pull away from your mouth and lay my head against your chest. Before I can stop them, the tears are flowing.

"Baby don't cry, please don't cry."

"You make me crazy. Why did you have to marry her? Her? After all you said? Why wouldn't you tell me? Fuck. You broke my heart! Y'all didn't have what we had. How could you?"

I'm pounding on his chest, as the tears are still falling.

"Wait. Broke your heart? What?"

I get quiet. You didn't have a clue.

"You love me?"

"Yes. I love you."

"Say it again."

"I love you."

You tilt my head up until I'm looking you in the eyes.

"I love you too."

I try to push away from you.

"Bianca don't go, I mean it. I mean every word I swear."

I stop, and you come up behind me, and kiss my neck and squeeze me tightly. You know I love it when you do that. You're sucking on my neck.

"You miss me?"

"Yes."

"I miss you too. I want to feel and taste that pussy. Come with me."

I follow you with my head down like the love-sick puppy I am. We go for a ride in your truck. You find this seemingly uninhabited dirt road. There are horses not far. We're up on a hill, and we can hear the horses making noises with our windows down.

"Get in the backseat and take your skirt and panties off."

I get out and get in the back seat and do what I'm told. My legs are open when you open the door.

"Damn I missed this pussy. "

You dive in head first, sucking my pussy and fingering me so confidently. You stop momentarily and take off your shirt and put it under me. You already know I'm about to wet this back seat up. As soon as you moan while sucking on my clit, it's waterworks everywhere. You're sucking my juices and swallowing them and it's making me wanna feel your dick inside me.

"Please, I need it deep inside. Fuck me."

Your face is coated with my cum, and you pull down your jogging pants, slide your dick in me, and kiss me simultaneously. I taste myself all on your tongue. I start sucking your tongue. You lift my legs to your shoulders, and start fucking me so fast and deep. All I can do is hold onto your shoulders and take everything you give. Ten strokes in and you start to slow down.

"Fuck, I should've cut the damn air on."

"Let me get on top."

You look at me with a smirk.

"You wanna ride daddy dick?"

"Please?"

We switch positions and as I put that dick inside me, I let out a deep sigh. I'd missed this fucking dick. I start going up and down, and holding on to the seat and your chest. Your face is sexy af from this angle. You stare at me, and we're both so into it.

"I'm so sorry baby. I'm sorry. It should've been you."

I look at you, roll my eyes, and place my hands on your neck. I start choking you as I ride you.

"This is my fucking dick. I'm gonna get this dick anytime I want. Fuck your wife. You hear me?"

I look down at you, and you nodd your head. I slap you.

"Damn girl."

"Say it."

"This your dick, and you can get it when you want."

"You promise?"

He pauses, and looks in my eyes.

"I promise."

I put my hands back around his throat and remember that we're in the backseat of your truck. I get on my tip toes, leave one hand around your neck as you get in a sitting position and put your arms around me. I'm taking you deeper inside me with each thrust. I'm still upset, but I'm also in need of this nut. It feels like a hate fuck almost. I'm giving you everything I have. I'm squeezing your big black curved dick for dear life. You're moaning under me. You're squeezing my ass tightly. Fuck. What the fuck, is all I hear you say, over and over again. Before I can register what's happening, you grip me tightly, and reposition me on my back. In one smooth motion, my legs are on your shoulders and you're deep inside me. You're fucking me so fast and I'm trying to match your rhythm, but I feel my release coming and the way you're staring in my eyes, with this crazy look, I know you aren't far behind me. You're giving me absolutely every inch of your big black curved dick, and it's hitting everything that's been neglected inside me. I close my eyes as it washes over me, and my body reacts on its own. I clamp down tightly on your dick and shoulders, and you grow bigger inside me. You shoot your release inside me and I coat your dick with my cream. It drips down your shaft, to your balls, and we both get untangled. We're trying to catch our breath, when headlights start coming our way.

"Fuckkkk" you say.

"Babe we gotta go."

We both hurry to put our clothes on. A truck with these red neck looking white guys, pull up beside us.

"Y'all can't be here. It's private property."

You throw your hand up at them and wave. You climb into the front seat and start the truck. Once I'm completely dressed, I climb through and sit on the passenger side. We look at each other and laugh.

You drive me back to my car. We kiss slowly and passionately. I get out and head to my car. You get out too, and you stop me. You pull me close in a tight hug. The tears start forming in the wells of my eyes, but I'm determined not to let them fall.

"You'll see me again soon, I promise ok?"

I nod my head, and you kiss me on my forehead. We both get I our vehicles and drive away.

Chapter 9

Possibilities

I was so excited about being off from work for the next two weeks. I'd taken the week off for Thanksgiving and the week afterwards. That insurance company could do without me for two weeks. Even though I was the best underwriter they had. Most of my coworkers had kids, so they preferred to be off around Christmas and the summertime. Thanksgiving was my favorite holiday. I did enjoy seeing family, but it was the change of seasons and the weather that I loved the most. Oh, and the food. I'd chosen to forego staying with relatives and I'd gotten a cute lil cabin not too far from Stone Mountain, Georgia. The pictures on the AirBnB app were cute, so I thought I'd enjoy myself. Georgia has always been home for me. I was born and raised there. I'd moved to Tampa, Florida after college. It was fine, but it was never too much of a change in weather seasons. It was either hot, rainy, a lil chilly, or too fucking hot. I missed Georgia for that very reason. I had boots that I could never wear in Florida. I'd packed them all too. I was definitely going to get some kind of wear out of them. Usually I drove up to my moms, but this year I didn't wanna do all that driving. I was catching the red eye Saturday night and planning to have some me time before Thanksgiving. I landed about 2 am Sunday. I was dog tired and glad I'd let the AirBnB hosts know I'd be there early. I went directly there with hardly any traffic and I was grateful. The temperature definitely was different here. It was probably around 40 degrees. I put the code in and was so grateful that it was warm inside. I put my bags down, stripped down, took a quick shower, peeked at the hot tub out back and knocked out.

I woke up around 1pm starving. Brunch sounded good. I grabbed my phone and Googled nearby places that served brunch. It was a place a few minutes from me, that served a buffet for brunch. They had sweet potato waffles, cheese grits, homemade biscuits, greens, and all kinds of southern cooking. All the reviews were good. I definitely was going there. I took my time in the shower this time. This water pressure was everything. I put on some jeans, a cute t-shirt and a ripped black sweater. I was glad I packed my black boots. I was cute today. I had my locs half up, half down. I put on my gold accessories I'd purchased from this black boutique on IG. I pulled up in no time, and the place was packed. I was still able to get a table rather quickly. They seated me near the windows at the back, and I wasn't far from this handsome guy in a gray sweater. He looked up at me and smiled. I smiled back and headed to the buffet. Everything looked and smelled so good. I settled on cheese grits, which are my favorite, home fries, fried fish, sweet potato biscuits, collard greens and fruit. I wanted to taste everything.

"Did you leave some for me?"

I looked up, and it's Mr. Handsome smiling at me. I looked down at my plate and shook my head.

"Not hardly."

We both laughed.

"Mind if I join you?"

I look up at this beautiful black man, and it's his eyes. They're captivating. For some reason, they have a sadness in them that it seems he's trying to hide.

"Sure."

When he brings his plate and drink over and sits down, I'm really able to get a good look at him. Bald, some gray in his beard, soft lips, long eyelashes, about 5'10", (we were basically the same height) nice muscled arms with tattoos on both. He was dressed nice. Creased jeans, oxford shoes that matched his sweater, manicured hands with short nails, no polish, no rings, but he had on a nice watch that looked expensive and he smelled like Creed, I think. Nice. He had the sleeves of his sweater up like he wasn't cold. I had to ask.

"Aren't you cold?"

"Nah, not at all. It feels good to me."

I raise my eyebrow and shake my head, and start digging in. No time to be all cute, I'm starving.

"It's nice seeing a woman that doesn't mind eating in front of me."

I swallow and look at him.

"I'm starving. I hadn't eaten since yesterday at lunch."

He laughs and I'm still checking him out. He is very attractive. We look in each other's eyes at the same time. Something changes between us in the moment. I'm more aware of him, his energy, and just how long it's been since I had sex. I can tell he's checking me out too.

"I'm Nate."

"I'm Niya ."

"Nice to meet you Niya."

"You as well."

We continue eating our food, and glancing at each other, and smiling. After a little bit, I'm stuffed, and I push my plate away. He's openly staring at me, and not trying to hide it.

"What? What is it?"

"I apologize for staring, but you're just really beautiful."

I know that I'm definitely blushing now. I stand up and excuse myself and head to the bathroom. I'm mentally chastising myself for getting turned on by a random guy that I've never met. I don't even know what possessed me to let him sit with me. But I figured it was a public place and I didn't really wanna eat alone. When I come back to the table, he isn't there. I look around, and I still don't see him. I look back at the table for both of our bills, and they aren't there. I find a waitress and she says that my bill was already paid. Well, that was nice of him. It'd be weird of me not to thank him. I smell him before I turn around.

"I was in the restroom. Were you waiting on me?"

"I... I just wanted to thank you for brunch. I didn't know you were gonna do that. You didn't have to."

"It's nothing. I wanted to."

"Well thanks, I really appreciate it."

It gets awkward for a second. I feel like I'm at the end of a date, and I don't know whether to hug him or shake his hand. Thankfully, he extends his hand, and I shake it.

"It was really nice meeting you Niya. Maybe we'll run into each other again."

I don't see how that's likely, so I just smile and wave. He walks around the corner, and I go in the opposite direction to the rental car I have. I hadn't decided if I wanted to shop first or last. As I get in the car, I decide that I'll wait to shop. No sense in shopping now, when Black Friday was coming up. I go through my screenshots and find the ranch I was looking for, put the address in the gps and head that way. For as long as I could remember, I've loved horses. I always thought it was perfect to go horseback riding in the fall. The heat and humidity in Florida had me concerned about the safety of the horses and with me working so much, I didn't go as often as I'd like to. I'd found this place one night when I couldn't sleep. Pulling up to it was a beautiful sight. It wasn't crowded at all. I put my phone in my back pocket and headed to pay. It was a family owned ranch and they were pleasant enough. I was walking out towards the horses when this beautiful Friesian caught my eye. He looked majestic standing there, with the wind blowing his hair. I walked up to him. I just had to touch him.

"He caught my eye too."

I'm shocked that it's Nate. Where did he come from? Did he follow me?

"Where'd you come from? You're not following me, are you?"

He laughs and shakes his head.

"Nah love, I come here when I'm down this way. They know me well."

Right at that moment, one of the handlers walks up.

"You decided the one you want today Nate? Raven again?"

"I think this young lady has her eyes on that one. I'll go with the pinto one there. That's Dale, right?"

"Yep that's him. I'll get them saddled for you both."

"How often do you come here?"

"Probably 6 or 7 times a year. What about you?"

"This is my first time coming here. I've been horseback riding before, but just not here."

"You're in for a treat. They have a big piece of land out here. We'll be crossing a few brooks and going up and down a few hills. Is that ok with you?"

"Of course. I love all that."

The handler has our horses saddled in no time, The tag above his chest says Bob. We both get on our own perspective horses and Bob mounts his. He leads the way and it was a beautiful experience. I was a little fearful going through the water and going up and down the hills, especially when Raven decided he was thirsty right in the middle of crossing. I guess the fear showed on my face.

"Pull his reins lightly and let him know it's not time to stop." Nate said.

I was grateful for him being there. As we headed back to the ranch, Nate and I were side by side. I was comfortable around him. The conversation flowed smoothly. The pauses didn't make me apprehensive. Weirdly, just like Georgia, Nate felt like home. That thought popped into my head, and it momentarily confused me. Felt like home? Never one to hide the emotions on my face, I guess he noticed my reaction.

"You ok?"

"Yeah i'm good. Just a random thought."

"From your face, it looked serious. Was it a bad thought?"

"Not at all. Just a puzzling one."

He looked at me, and just smiled.

"I won't push. You'll share it with me when you're ready."

Who did this joker think he is? Showing up in my life looking all good, acting like he knew me or something. That made me smirk a little. Whatever was happening, I was enjoying it. I hadn't had this much fun in a while. When I finally dismounted from Raven, my thighs were sore. I felt like I was walking gap legged to my car. Nate was beside me, and by the looks of things, his walk hadn't changed much. He definitely did this more than me. He was parked two cars away from mine. This time he walked me to my car.

"It's funny we ran into each other again."

"Yeah, I just knew you were stalking me."

"Is it out of line for me to say that I still wanna spend more time with you?"

"Well... no. I don't think it's out of line. A little unorthodox maybe, but we're adults."

No sooner than I said those words, it's like my body began to wake up.

"Where are you headed to now?"

"Just back to my AirBnB. I'll maybe relax a little bit, maybe the rest of the day, it just depends on how I feel. I'm still kind of thrown off from that flight. What about you?"

"I was headed back to the Marriott for a little relaxing myself. But before I go, would it be ok if I gave you my number?"

"Sure. I'd like that."

I hand him my phone and he puts his number in. I didn't recognize the 732 area code but I shrug it off. He says he'll be looking to hear from me soon. We both smile and get into our vehicles and go our separate ways.

I'm back at the cabin and I'm exhausted. I strip off all my clothes, and I wanna just soak. I run a bath and think about the hot tub. I'm definitely going to try it out before I leave. As I'm running the water, I put on my it's a vibe playlist and decide that I'm not going anywhere else today. I'm more worn out than I think. I add some oil, rose petals and bath bombs to my bath. This tub is beautiful and spacious. All white in the middle of the bathroom. The shower is all clear glass with double shower heads. I soak long enough to have pruned skin. I let the water out, get in the shower and wash the day away. Once I'm out I put on my lace mustard teddy and black silk robe. I look at myself in the floor length mirror, and wanna touch myself. I put on my pineapple body butter that was all natural. I'd got it from a small black owned company I'd found on Instagram. It smelled delicious. I put it all over me and it makes my skin glow and feel so smooth. He pops in my mind and I'm wondering what he's doing. I decide that I want the attention, so I do something so unorthodox for me. I pick up my phone and call him.

"Hello."

His voice makes me bite my lip.

"Hi, it's Niya."

"I'm glad you called Niya. I was wondering if you would."

"Honestly, I wasn't sure if I was going to."

"What made you do it?"

"I didn't wanna be alone tonight. So, I thought I'd see if you felt the same way."

He hesitates for a second.

"If we're being honest, I didn't wanna leave your side earlier. I just thought I'd come off as too pushy if I said that out loud. It may sound crazy, but I like being with you."

"Do you have plans for tonight?"

"Nah, I just got out of the shower. I was gonna just relax, and maybe go down to the bar for a drink."

"What if you had that drink over here?"

"Sounds like a plan. Send me the address and I'm on my way."

I send him the address and go make sure it's enough wine and liquor to share. I'm wondering if I should change my clothes. I look down at myself. If I'm dressed like this, he's going to think I'm ready to fuck. My robe covers everything though, so I'll just keep it pulled tight. In the back of my mind, I'm wondering if I am going to fuck him. He is sexy. But I hardly know him. My body deserved this though. I needed it. I don't have to know him to fuck him. I'm a grown ass woman with needs. I smile to myself. Well that settles that. He pulls up in no time and when he knocks, I close my robe and put my feet in my fur slippers. I open the door and he just stares at me.

"Wow you look nice."

"Thanks, come in out of the cold. What are you drinking?"

"Cognac on the rocks, if you have it."

"I do. I'll be right back. Put your coat over there on that rack and have a seat, or you could look around."

He chooses to look around as I go pour his drink.

"This is really nice. I need to AirBnB it next time. That's a nice-looking hot tub. You been in it yet?"

"Not yet. I want to before I leave though."

"There is a storm coming, it's supposed to be snowing by morning."

"Really? I need to start watching the weather. I don't watch TV and get most of my updates from social media."

"Yep, we're supposed to get 3 to 4 inches."

"Wow, I haven't seen snow since I was a child."

I bring him his drink, and I've made me a vodka and cranberry. We both go to the couch and he looks at me as he sips his drink.

"I'm glad you called."

"So am I."

"So, what are you into Niya? Like with men, sexually? What are your interests?"

I laugh. "You're just gonna jump into it I see. I'm into different things. I'm versatile. I like to be submissive and I like to be dominant sometimes too. I'm open to almost anything."

He takes a sip of his drink, and smiles.

"I like that."

"Do you? Why is that?"

"I like to be dominated."

It was my turn to take a sip of my drink. I think I actually gulp it. Well well well. I was about to get exactly what I needed. I look over at him, and his drink is almost gone.

"Want another one?"

"Sure. While you fix it, show me where your bathroom is."

"No problem. It's down the hall and to the left."

He gets up and heads that way. I fix his drink, put it where he was sitting and head to the closet. I change into my heels and take my robe off. I dig around in my bag for a few essential things. I was always prepared. You never knew when you'd have time to play. I dimmed the lights some. He comes back and his face lights up.

"This is what I'm talking about."

He picks up his drink and takes a long sip.

"Take off your clothes and get on your knees."

He looks at me and does exactly what I ask. I stand there watching him, and I'm enjoying every minute. He's not in a rush at all. He's completely naked now, and he gets on his knees. I walk over to him and touch his back lightly.

"So you like being dominated huh, we'll see about that. What don't you like? What can't I do to you?"

"I don't want anything in my ass. Everything else is a go."

I smirk at him.

"No pegging? Well that's a shame. But I can work with that."

I lightly graze his head with my nails, as I walk around him.

"You are to refer to me as Mistress from this second on. Do you understand?"

"Yes mistress."

"Open your mouth and stick out your tongue."

I'm standing in front of him. He sticks his tongue out, and I put my pussy in his face. His tongue is on my lace teddy, and I'm feeling his breath against my pussy.

"Do you like the way my pussy smells?"

"Fuck yes Mistress, I wanna taste it—"

I grab his throat tightly. He looks up at me, eyes full of desire, and I notice his dick getting hard.

"You do what I say. You taste it when I say so. Understood?"

"Yes Mistress."

I feel my pussy starting to throb. A lil taste won't hurt. I reach down and unsnap the crotch of the teddy.

"Lick your tongue out again."

He does just that. I grab the back of his head and push his face into my pussy. He's licking and slurping everywhere.

"Lick and suck on that clit and slow it down."

His warm breath and soft tongue feel so good on my clit. I'm still holding his head steady, and after a few minutes, I feel myself getting weak standing like this.

"Crawl over here."

I go sit in the chair and open my legs wide. I open my pussy lips as he gets close. He puts his face between my legs, and I put one hand on his head.

"Suck that fucking clit."

He's sucking it and it feels so good. I know i'm gonna cum soon. I pull his head up and tell him to stick his tongue out. I scoot down in the chair.

"Tongue fuck my pussy."

He goes crazy, and he's moaning as his tongue is going deep inside my pussy.

"Don't you fucking stop. I'm going to cum down your fucking throat."

My legs are shaking, my toes are crunching up inside these red heels. His moans and eagerness to follow directions is everything to me. When I feel my release coming, I grab his head, and put it in the exact position I need it in.

"You better get every fucking drop too."

It comes out of me in a rush and he's trying to catch it all.

"Swallow it all. Suck the cum out of me. Every fucking drop. Now. Don't stop until you've cleaned up this mess I've made all you're your face, and this chair. Fuck."

My body convulses and I jerk with every lick. He does just as I asked. I lessen up my hold on his head some. He starts licking my pussy softly. When I'm able to move, I tell him to get up and walk in the room. I pull my teddy over my head and leave it on the couch. I keep the heels on. He's standing by the bed when I walk in. I walk behind him and tie his hands behind his back. Good thing I'd bought those zip ties.

"Mistress, what the fuck, you sure?"

"Are you questioning me?"

"No Mistress."

"Good. Hush."

I turn him to me and kiss him slowly. My pussy tastes so good on his lips. He relaxes against me. The look in his eyes says he trusts me. I push him away from the bed and into the love seat. He falls with a thud and we both laugh. I get on my knees in front of him. He's watching me with piqued interest.

"You want me to suck it?"

"Fuck yes Mistress."

I laugh.

"You haven't done well enough to deserve head, yet. Lick your tongue out."

He licks his tongue out and I turn around, spread my legs, and hold my ass cheeks open.

"Let's see how well you eat this ass."

I back all the way up on his face, and I feel his nose and lips. He's inhaling my scent, and I'm loving it. He slowly licks my ass, and it's not enough for me.

"If you wanna cum tonight, you need to eat this ass correctly. You need to make me cum again. You'd better go deep too."

He stops the soft licking and eats my ass just as well as he ate my pussy, all with his hands tied behind his back.

"Tongue fuck my ass. Make me cum again. You're a nasty bitch and I love it."

He puts his tongue deep in my ass, and I grab the clit sucker I had on the love seat. I put it directly on my clit and turn it up. In seconds I'm ready to explode. I leave one hand on the clit sucker and I put the other on his head.

"Don't you stop. Don't you fucking stop."

My body goes limp as I cream everywhere. He's taking his tongue and lapping up the cream and takes turns licking my pussy cream and tongue fucking my ass. My clit and pussy are so sensitive that I push his face away. I can't take anymore sensation right now. I look down and his dick is so hard. He does deserve to cum now. He's looking up at me with a wet shiny face, and those fucking eyes. Those sexy ass eyes that seem like they're begging me. Damn. I drop to my knees. I put his dick in my mouth, and I'm sucking it with everything I have. I don't want him to cum this way yet so after I've wet the dick up good, I stop. He looks at me in shock, but he wisely says nothing. I get up off the floor and come and sit astride him. I put his dick inside me. We both sigh. I put my hands on his shoulders.

"Fuck. I needed this. Stop being quiet and talk to me."

His eyes light up when I say that.

"Fuck me Mistress. Put that fat pussy on me. You so fucking wet. I wanna have your pussy and ass on my tongue all the time. You taste so good. Please Mistress, fuck me. Punish me."

The heels are digging into the love seat and I pick up speed. Being able to control this is so satisfying. I just know his arms are about to cramp up, but this is so good. Plus, he did say punish him. I look down at him and I kiss him. We're in sync with our movements. His dick is about 6 inches with a slight curve, but it's so damn thick. My pussy is thanking me right now. I slow it down and start fucking him slow and looking in his eyes. I wanna do something I haven't done in a while. His eyes tell me yes, before I even do it. I stop moving and get off his dick. I stand, turn my back to him, and ease my ass onto his dick. As soon as it's at my asshole, we both hold our breath for a second. Once it glides inside, we exhale. It feels so damn good. His dick is the perfect size for anal. Me having control makes it that much better. I was able to do what felt best for me, and that's what I needed.

"Mistress this tight asshole gonna make me cum."

"Did I say you could cum?"

"Please Mistress, let me cum. I need it. Please."

"I'll allow it this time, you have been obedient."

"Thank you, Mistress. Where would you like me to cum?"

"Fill up my ass with it, cum while you're deep inside this ass."

"Fuck. Yes Mistress."

I feel his dick throbbing inside my ass. I turn my head and kiss him. He does just as I asked and fills my ass up with cum. So much so that I feel it leaking out of me. I should make him lick it up, but I'm exhausted with this dominate play. I remember that his hands are tied behind his back. I let him free, and I just know he's gonna have bruises. Good thing it's cold up here and hopefully his wrists will stay covered. He takes my face, holds it and kisses me softly. We're both drained and we get into the bed. Not long after we hit the sheets, we're both out.

In the middle of the night, the storm wakes us up. My back is still to him. He pulls me closer and kisses me. I feel his dick getting hard against my ass. He lifts my ass cheek up, and slides right into my pussy. He continues to kiss me as he fucks me. He puts one arm around my neck as he kisses me. His dick sliding in and out of me feels so good. I turn my head towards the pillow. He puts pressure on my neck, and I love it. He's fucking me deep and doing everything he couldn't last night.

"I wanna cum deep inside this pussy. You gonna let me?"

"Why? You wanna be a single father?"

We both laugh. He smacks my ass and pulls my body closer to his.

"Fuck me, fuck me."

His stroke goes into overdrive after I say that. My body is going forward with each stroke. I'm throwing it back as hard as he's giving it.

"Mistress tell me where you want me to cum."

I hesitate for a second.

"Cum inside me."

We both stop moving.

"Are you sure?"

"You're questioning me?"

He kisses me and resumes fucking me. He's so deep inside.

"Cum inside of me. I need it. Please."

His dick throbs deep inside me. He shakes and moans and fills my pussy up with his cum. He looks me in my eyes, as I lay on my back.

"Can you stay?"

"Yeah I can stay. My flight is in two days."

"Where are you going?"

"Back home. I was here for business."

"Where's home?"

"New Jersey. Where are you flying in from?"

"Florida."

"Florida? Damn. I didn't know that. I don't care though. I'm not letting you go that easily. You're too special for that.

I look at him and arch my eyebrow.

"You're not letting me go?"

"Nah. We'll figure it out. We can make this work if we want to. Don't

we owe it to ourselves to try?"

I stare into his eyes and I hope and I dream of the possibilities.

Made in the USA
Columbia, SC
17 December 2020